# The Black Poodle & Other Tales by F. Anstey

F. Anstey was the pseudonym of Thomas Anstey Guthrie who was born in Kensington, London on August 8th, 1856, to Augusta Amherst Austen, an organist and composer, and Thomas Anstey Guthrie., a prosperous military tailor

Anstey was educated at King's College School and then at Trinity Hall, Cambridge. Although his education was first rate Anstey could only manage a third-class degree; A Gentlemen's degree as it was euphemistically known.

In 1880 he was called to the bar. However this career path rapidly fell away in his desire to become an author. The successful publication of Vice Versa, in 1882, with the premise of a substitution of a father for his schoolboy son, made his name and reputation as a refreshing and original humorist.

The following year he published a rather more serious work, The Giant's Robe. Interestingly the story is about a plagiarist and Anstey was, ironically, accused of plagiarism in writing the work. Despite good reviews both he and his public knew that his writing career was to be that of a humorist.

In the following years he published prolifically beginning with; The Black Poodle (1884), The Tinted Venus (1885), A Fallen Idol (1886), and Baboo Jabberjee B.A. (1897).

Anstey worked not only as a novelist and short story writer but was also a valued member of the staff at the humorous Punch magazine, in which his voces populi and his parodies of a reciter's stock-piece (Burglar Bill) represent perhaps his best work.

In 1901, his successful farce, The Man from Blankleys, based on a story that originally appeared in Punch, was first produced on stage at the Prince of Wales Theatre, in London.

Anstey had become a writer, and a successful one at that, of many talents.

Many more of his stories were made into plays and films over the years. Others were simply taken for the premise alone, usually with no credit to the original author.

By the end of the First World War Anstey's original publications had slowed to a crawl and he seemed rather more interested in translating and publishing some works of Moliere.

Thomas Anstey Guthrie died of pneumonia on March 10th, 1934 in London.

His self-deprecating autobiography, A Long Retrospect, was published in 1936.

## Index of Contents
THE BLACK POODLE
THE STORY OF A SUGAR PRINCE
THE RETURN OF AGAMEMNON
THE WRAITH OF BARNJUM
A TOY TRAGEDY

AN UNDERGRADUATE'S AUNT
THE SIREN
THE CURSE OF THE CATAFALQUES
A FAREWELL APPEARANCE
ACCOMPANIED ON THE FLUTE
F. ANSTEY – A CONCISE BIBLIOGRAPHY

## THE BLACK POODLE

I have set myself the task of relating in the course of this story, without suppressing or altering a single detail, the most painful and humiliating episode in my life.

I do this, not because it will give me the least pleasure, but simply because it affords me an opportunity of extenuating myself which has hitherto been wholly denied to me.

As a general rule I am quite aware that to publish a lengthy explanation of one's conduct in any questionable transaction is not the best means of recovering a lost reputation; but in my own case there is one to whom I shall never more be permitted to justify myself by word of mouth—even if I found myself able to attempt it. And as she could not possibly think worse of me than she does at present, I write this, knowing it can do me no harm, and faintly hoping that it may come to her notice and suggest a doubt whether I am quite so unscrupulous a villain, so consummate a hypocrite, as I have been forced to appear in her eyes.

The bare chance of such a result makes me perfectly indifferent to all else: I cheerfully expose to the derision of the whole reading world the story of my weakness and my shame, since by doing so I may possibly rehabilitate myself somewhat in the good opinion of one person.

Having said so much, I will begin my confession without further delay:—

My name is Algernon Weatherhead, and I may add that I am in one of the Government departments; that I am an only son, and live at home with my mother.

We had had a house at Hammersmith until just before the period covered by this history, when, our lease expiring, my mother decided that my health required country air at the close of the day, and so we took a 'desirable villa residence' on one of the many new building estates which have lately sprung up in such profusion in the home counties.

We have called it 'Wistaria Villa.' It is a pretty little place, the last of a row of detached villas, each with its tiny rustic carriage gate and gravel sweep in front, and lawn enough for a tennis court behind, which lines the road leading over the hill to the railway station.

I could certainly have wished that our landlord, shortly after giving us the agreement, could have found some other place to hang himself in than one of our attics, for the consequence was that a housemaid left us in violent hysterics about every two months, having learnt the tragedy from the tradespeople, and naturally 'seen a somethink' immediately afterwards.

Still it is a pleasant house, and I can now almost forgive the landlord for what I shall always consider an act of gross selfishness on his part.

In the country, even so near town, a next-door neighbour is something more than a mere numeral; he is a possible acquaintance, who will at least consider a new-comer as worth the experiment of a call. I soon knew that 'Shuturgarden,' the next house to our own, was occupied by a Colonel Currie, a retired Indian officer; and often, as across the low boundary wall I caught a glimpse of a graceful girlish figure flitting about amongst the rose-bushes in the neighbouring garden, I would lose myself in pleasant anticipations of a time not far distant when the wall which separated us would be (metaphorically) levelled.

I remember—ah, how vividly!—the thrill of excitement with which I heard from my mother on returning from town one evening that the Curries had called, and seemed disposed to be all that was neighbourly and kind.

I remember, too, the Sunday afternoon on which I returned their call—alone, as my mother had already done so during the week. I was standing on the steps of the Colonel's villa waiting for the door to open when I was startled by a furious snarling and yapping behind, and, looking round, discovered a large poodle in the act of making for my legs.

He was a coal-black poodle, with half of his right ear gone, and absurd little thick moustaches at the end of his nose; he was shaved in the sham-lion fashion, which is considered, for some mysterious reason, to improve a poodle, but the barber had left sundry little tufts of hair which studded his haunches capriciously.

I could not help being reminded, as I looked at him, of another black poodle which Faust entertained for a short time, with unhappy results, and I thought that a very moderate degree of incantation would be enough to bring the fiend out of this brute.

He made me intensely uncomfortable, for I am of a slightly nervous temperament, with a constitutional horror of dogs and a liability to attacks of diffidence on performing the ordinary social rites under the most favourable conditions, and certainly the consciousness that a strange and apparently savage dog was engaged in worrying the heels of my boots was the reverse of reassuring.

The Currie family received me with all possible kindness: 'So charmed to make your acquaintance, Mr. Weatherhead,' said Mrs. Currie, as I shook hands. 'I see,' she added pleasantly, 'you've brought the doggie in with you.' As a matter of fact, I had brought the doggie in at the ends of my coat-tails, but it was evidently no unusual occurrence for visitors to appear in this undignified manner, for she detached him quite as a matter of course, and, as soon as I was sufficiently collected, we fell into conversation.

I discovered that the Colonel and his wife were childless, and the slender willowy figure I had seen across the garden wall was that of Lilian Roseblade, their niece and adopted daughter. She came into the room shortly afterwards, and I felt, as I went through the form of an introduction, that her sweet fresh face, shaded by soft masses of dusky brown hair, more than justified all the dreamy hopes and fancies with which I had looked forward to that moment.

She talked to me in a pretty, confidential, appealing way, which I have heard her dearest friends censure as childish and affected, but I thought then that her manner had an indescribable charm and fascination about it, and the memory of it makes my heart ache now with a pang that is not all pain.

Even before the Colonel made his appearance I had begun to see that my enemy, the poodle, occupied an exceptional position in that household. It was abundantly clear by the time I took my leave.

He seemed to be the centre of their domestic system, and even lovely Lilian revolved contentedly around him as a kind of satellite; he could do no wrong in his owner's eyes, his prejudices (and he was a narrow-minded animal) were rigorously respected, and all domestic arrangements were made with a primary view to his convenience.

I may be wrong, but I cannot think that it is wise to put any poodle upon such a pedestal as that. How this one in particular, as ordinary a quadruped as ever breathed, had contrived to impose thus upon his infatuated proprietors, I never could understand, but so it was—he even engrossed the chief part of the conversation, which after any lull seemed to veer round to him by a sort of natural law.

I had to endure a long biographical sketch of him—what a Society paper would call an 'anecdotal photo'—and each fresh anecdote seemed to me to exhibit the depraved malignity of the beast in a more glaring light, and render the doting admiration of the family more astounding than ever.

'Did you tell Mr. Weatherhead, Lily, about Bingo' (Bingo was the poodle's preposterous name) 'and Tacks? No? Oh, I must tell him that—it'll make him laugh. Tacks is our gardener down in the village (d'ye know Tacks?). Well, Tacks was up here the other day, nailing up some trellis-work at the top of a ladder, and all the time there was Master Bingo sitting quietly at the foot of it looking on, wouldn't leave it on any account. Tacks said he was quite company for him. Well, at last, when Tacks had finished and was coming down, what do you think that rascal there did? Just sneaked quietly up behind and nipped him in both calves and ran off. Been looking out for that the whole time! Ha, ha!—deep that, eh?'

I agreed with an inward shudder that it was very deep, thinking privately that, if this was a specimen of Bingo's usual treatment of the natives, it would be odd if he did not find himself deeper still before—probably just before—he died.

'Poor faithful old doggie!' murmured Mrs. Currie; 'he thought Tacks was a nasty burglar, didn't he? he wasn't going to see Master robbed, was he?'

'Capital house-dog, sir,' struck in the Colonel. 'Gad, I shall never forget how he made poor Heavisides run for it the other day! Ever met Heavisides of the Bombay Fusiliers? Well, Heavisides was staying here, and the dog met him one morning as he was coming down from the bath-room. Didn't recognise him in "pyjamas" and a dressing-gown, of course, and made at him. He kept poor old Heavisides outside the landing window on the top of the cistern for a quarter of an hour, till I had to come and raise the siege!'

Such were the stories of that abandoned dog's blunderheaded ferocity to which I was forced to listen, while all the time the brute sat opposite me on the hearthrug, blinking at me from under his shaggy mane with his evil bleared eyes, and deliberating where he would have me when I rose to go.

This was the beginning of an intimacy which soon displaced all ceremony. It was very pleasant to go in there after dinner, even to sit with the Colonel over his claret and hear more stories about Bingo, for afterwards I could go into the pretty drawing-room and take my tea from Lilian's hands, and listen while she played Schubert to us in the summer twilight.

The poodle was always in the way, to be sure, but even his ugly black head seemed to lose some of its ugliness and ferocity when Lilian laid her pretty hand on it.

On the whole I think that the Currie family were well disposed towards me; the Colonel considering me as a harmless specimen of the average eligible young man—which I certainly was—and Mrs. Currie showing me favour for my mother's sake, for whom she had taken a strong liking.

As for Lilian, I believed I saw that she soon suspected the state of my feelings towards her and was not displeased by it. I looked forward with some hopefulness to a day when I could declare myself with no fear of a repulse.

But it was a serious obstacle in my path that I could not secure Bingo's good opinion on any terms. The family would often lament this pathetically themselves. 'You see,' Mrs. Currie would observe in apology, 'Bingo is a dog that does not attach himself easily to strangers'—though for that matter I thought he was unpleasantly ready to attach himself to me.

I did try hard to conciliate him. I brought him propitiatory buns—which was weak and ineffectual, as he ate them with avidity, and hated me as bitterly as ever, for he had conceived from the first a profound contempt for me and a distrust which no blandishments of mine could remove. Looking back now, I am inclined to think it was a prophetic instinct that warned him of what was to come upon him through my instrumentality.

Only his approbation was wanting to establish for me a firm footing with the Curries, and perhaps determine Lilian's wavering heart in my direction; but, though I wooed that inflexible poodle with an assiduity I blush to remember, he remained obstinately firm.

Still, day by day, Lilian's treatment of me was more encouraging; day by day I gained in the esteem of her uncle and aunt; I began to hope that soon I should be able to disregard canine influence altogether.

Now there was one inconvenience about our villa (besides its flavour of suicide) which it is necessary to mention here. By common consent all the cats of the neighbourhood had selected our garden for their evening reunions. I fancy that a tortoiseshell kitchen cat of ours must have been a sort of leader of local feline society—I know she was 'at home,' with music and recitations, on most evenings.

My poor mother found this interfered with her after-dinner nap, and no wonder, for if a cohort of ghosts had been 'shrieking and squealing,' as Calpurnia puts it, in our back garden, or it had been fitted up as a crèche for a nursery of goblin infants in the agonies of teething, the noise could not possibly have been more unearthly.

We sought for some means of getting rid of the nuisance: there was poison of course, but we thought it would have an invidious appearance, and even lead to legal difficulties, if each dawn were to discover an assortment of cats expiring in hideous convulsions in various parts of the same garden.

Firearms, too, were open to objection, and would scarcely assist my mother's slumbers, so for some time we were at a loss for a remedy. At last, one day, walking down the Strand, I chanced to see (in an evil hour) what struck me as the very thing—it was an air-gun of superior construction displayed in a gunsmith's window. I went in at once, purchased it, and took it home in triumph; it would be noiseless, and would reduce the local average of cats without scandal—one or two examples, and feline fashion would soon migrate to a more secluded spot.

I lost no time in putting this to the proof. That same evening I lay in wait after dusk at the study window, protecting my mother's repose. As soon as I heard the long-drawn wail, the preliminary sputter, and the wild stampede that followed, I let fly in the direction of the sound. I suppose I must have something of the national sporting instinct in me, for my blood was tingling with excitement; but the feline constitution assimilates lead without serious inconvenience, and I began to fear that no trophy would remain to bear witness to my marksmanship.

But all at once I made out a dark indistinct form slinking in from behind the bushes. I waited till it crossed a belt of light which streamed from the back kitchen below me, and then I took careful aim and pulled the trigger.

This time at least I had not failed—there was a smothered yell, a rustle—and then silence again. I ran out with the calm pride of a successful revenge to bring in the body of my victim, and I found underneath a laurel, no predatory tom-cat, but (as the discerning reader will no doubt have foreseen long since) the quivering carcase of the Colonel's black poodle!

I intend to set down here the exact unvarnished truth, and I confess that at first, when I knew what I had done, I was not sorry. I was quite innocent of any intention of doing it, but I felt no regret. I even laughed—madman that I was—at the thought that there was the end of Bingo at all events; that impediment was removed, my weary task of conciliation was over for ever!

But soon the reaction came; I realised the tremendous nature of my deed, and shuddered. I had done that which might banish me from Lilian's side for ever! All unwittingly I had slaughtered a kind of sacred beast, the animal around which the Currie household had wreathed their choicest affections! How was I to break it to them? Should I send Bingo in with a card tied to his neck and my regrets and compliments? That was too much like a present of game. Ought I not to carry him in myself? I would wreathe him in the best crape, I would put on black for him—the Curries would hardly consider a taper and a white sheet, or sackcloth and ashes, an excessive form of atonement—but I could not grovel to quite such an abject extent.

I wondered what the Colonel would say. Simple and hearty as a general rule, he had a hot temper on occasions, and it made me ill as I thought, would he and, worse still, would Lilian believe it was really an accident? They knew what an interest I had in silencing the deceased poodle—would they believe the simple truth?

I vowed that they should believe me. My genuine remorse and the absence of all concealment on my part would speak powerfully for me. I would choose a favourable time for my confession; that very evening I would tell all.

Still I shrank from the duty before me, and as I knelt down sorrowfully by the dead form and respectfully composed his stiffening limbs, I thought that it was unjust of Fate to place a well-meaning man, whose nerves were not of iron, in such a position.

Then, to my horror, I heard a well-known ringing tramp on the road outside, and smelt the peculiar fragrance of a Burmese cheroot. It was the Colonel himself, who had been taking out the doomed Bingo for his usual evening run.

I don't know how it was exactly, but a sudden panic came over me. I held my breath, and tried to crouch down unseen behind the laurels; but he had seen me, and came over at once to speak to me across the hedge.

He stood there, not two yards from his favourite's body! Fortunately it was unusually dark that evening.

'Ha, there you are, eh?' he began heartily; 'don't rise, my boy, don't rise.' I was trying to put myself in front of the poodle, and did not rise—at least, only my hair did.

'You're out late, ain't you?' he went on; 'laying out your garden, hey?'

I could not tell him that I was laying out his poodle! My voice shook as, with a guilty confusion that was veiled by the dusk, I said it was a fine evening—which it was not.

'Cloudy, sir,' said the Colonel, 'cloudy—rain before morning, I think. By the way, have you seen anything of my Bingo in here?'

This was the turning point. What I ought to have done was to say mournfully, 'Yes, I'm sorry to say I've had a most unfortunate accident with him—here he is—the fact is, I'm afraid I've shot him!'

But I couldn't. I could have told him at my own time, in a prepared form of words—but not then. I felt I must use all my wits to gain time and fence with the questions.

'Why,' I said with a leaden airiness, 'he hasn't given you the slip, has he?'

'Never did such a thing in his life!' said the Colonel, warmly; 'he rushed off after a rat or a frog or something a few minutes ago, and as I stopped to light another cheroot I lost sight of him. I thought I saw him slip in under your gate, but I've been calling him from the front there and he won't come out.'

No, and he never would come out any more. But the Colonel must not be told that just yet. I temporised again: 'If,' I said unsteadily, 'if he had slipped in under the gate, I should have seen him. Perhaps he took it into his head to run home?'

'Oh, I shall find him on the doorstep, I expect, the knowing old scamp! Why, what d'ye think was the last thing he did, now?'

I could have given him the very latest intelligence; but I dared not. However, it was altogether too ghastly to kneel there and laugh at anecdotes of Bingo told across Bingo's dead body; I could not stand that! 'Listen,' I said suddenly, 'wasn't that his bark? There again; it seems to come from the front of your house, don't you think?'

'Well,' said the Colonel, 'I'll go and fasten him up before he's off again. How your teeth are chattering—you've caught a chill, man—go indoors at once and, if you feel equal to it, look in half an hour later about grog time, and I'll tell you all about it. Compliments to your mother. Don't forget—about grog time!' I had got rid of him at last, and I wiped my forehead, gasping with relief. I would go round in half an hour, and then I should be prepared to make my melancholy announcement. For, even then, I never thought of any other course, until suddenly it flashed upon me with terrible clearness that my miserable shuffling by the hedge had made it impossible to tell the truth! I had not told a direct lie, to be sure, but then I had given the Colonel the impression that I had denied having seen the dog. Many people can appease their consciences by reflecting that, whatever may be the effect their words produce, they did contrive to steer clear of a downright lie. I never quite knew where the distinction lay, morally, but there is that feeling—I have it myself.

Unfortunately, prevarication has this drawback, that, if ever the truth comes to light, the prevaricator is in just the same case as if he had lied to the most shameless extent, and for a man to point out that the words he used contained no absolute falsehood will seldom restore confidence.

I might of course still tell the Colonel of my misfortune, and leave him to infer that it had happened after our interview, but the poodle was fast becoming cold and stiff, and they would most probably suspect the real time of the occurrence.

And then Lilian would hear that I had told a string of falsehoods to her uncle over the dead body of their idolised Bingo—an act, no doubt, of abominable desecration, of unspeakable profanity in her eyes!

If it would have been difficult before to prevail on her to accept a bloodstained hand, it would be impossible after that. No, I had burnt my ships, I was cut off for ever from the straightforward course; that one moment of indecision had decided my conduct in spite of me—I must go on with it now and keep up the deception at all hazards.

It was bitter. I had always tried to preserve as many of the moral principles which had been instilled into me as can be conveniently retained in this grasping world, and it had been my pride that, roughly speaking, I had never been guilty of an unmistakable falsehood.

But henceforth, if I meant to win Lilian, that boast must be relinquished for ever! I should have to lie now with all my might, without limit or scruple, to dissemble incessantly, and 'wear a mask,' as the poet Bunn beautifully expressed it long ago, 'over my hollow heart.' I felt all this keenly—I did not think it was right—but what was I to do?

After thinking all this out very carefully, I decided that my only course was to bury the poor animal where he fell and say nothing about it. With some vague idea of precaution I first took off the silver collar he wore, and then hastily interred him with a garden-trowel and succeeded in removing all traces of the disaster.

I fancy I felt a certain relief in the knowledge that there would now be no necessity to tell my pitiful story and risk the loss of my neighbours' esteem.

By-and-by, I thought, I would plant a rose-tree over his remains, and some day, as Lilian and I, in the noontide of our domestic bliss, stood before it admiring its creamy luxuriance, I might (perhaps) find courage to confess that the tree owed some of that luxuriance to the long-lost Bingo.

There was a touch of poetry in this idea that lightened my gloom for the moment.

I need scarcely say that I did not go round to Shuturgarden that evening. I was not hardened enough for that yet—my manner might betray me, and so I very prudently stayed at home.

But that night my sleep was broken by frightful dreams. I was perpetually trying to bury a great gaunt poodle, which would persist in rising up through the damp mould as fast as I covered him up.... Lilian and I were engaged, and we were in church together on Sunday, and the poodle, resisting all attempts to eject him, forbade our banns with sepulchral barks.... It was our wedding-day, and at the critical moment the poodle leaped between us and swallowed the ring.... Or we were at the wedding-breakfast, and Bingo, a grizzly black skeleton with flaming eyes, sat on the cake and would not allow Lilian to cut it. Even the rose-tree fancy was reproduced in a distorted form—the tree grew, and every blossom contained a miniature Bingo, which barked; and as I woke I was desperately trying to persuade the Colonel that they were ordinary dog-roses.

I went up to the office next day with my gloomy secret gnawing my bosom, and, whatever I did, the spectre of the murdered poodle rose before me. For two days after that I dared not go near the Curries, until at last one evening after dinner I forced myself to call, feeling that it was really not safe to keep away any longer.

My conscience smote me as I went in. I put on an unconscious easy manner, which was such a dismal failure that it was lucky for me that they were too much engrossed to notice it.

I never before saw a family so stricken down by a domestic misfortune as the group I found in the drawing-room, making a dejected pretence of reading or working. We talked at first—and hollow talk it was—on indifferent subjects, till I could bear it no longer, and plunged boldly into danger.

'I don't see the dog,' I began. 'I suppose you—you found him all right the other evening, Colonel?' I wondered as I spoke whether they would not notice the break in my voice, but they did not.

'Why, the fact is,' said the Colonel, heavily, gnawing his grey moustache, 'we've not heard anything of him since: he's—he's run off!'

'Gone, Mr. Weatherhead; gone without a word!' said Mrs. Currie, plaintively, as if she thought the dog might at least have left an address.

'I wouldn't have believed it of him,' said the Colonel; 'it has completely knocked me over. Haven't been so cut up for years—the ungrateful rascal!'

'Oh, Uncle!' pleaded Lilian, 'don't talk like that; perhaps Bingo couldn't help it—perhaps some one has s-s-shot him!'

'Shot!' cried the Colonel, angrily. 'By heaven! if I thought there was a villain on earth capable of shooting that poor inoffensive dog, I'd—Why should they shoot him, Lilian? Tell me that! I—I hope you won't let me hear you talk like that again. You don't think he's shot, eh, Weatherhead?'

I said—Heaven forgive me!—that I thought it highly improbable.

'He's not dead!' cried Mrs. Currie. 'If he were dead I should know it somehow—I'm sure I should! But I'm certain he's alive. Only last night I had such a beautiful dream about him. I thought he came back to us,

Mr. Weatherhead, driving up in a hansom cab, and he was just the same as ever—only he wore blue spectacles, and the shaved part of him was painted a bright red. And I woke up with the joy—so, you know, it's sure to come true!'

It will be easily understood what torture conversations like these were to me, and how I hated myself as I sympathised and spoke encouraging words concerning the dog's recovery, when I knew all the time he was lying hid under my garden mould. But I took it as a part of my punishment, and bore it all uncomplainingly; practice even made me an adept in the art of consolation—I believe I really was a great comfort to them.

I had hoped that they would soon get over the first bitterness of their loss, and that Bingo would be first replaced and then forgotten in the usual way; but there seemed no signs of this coming to pass.

The poor Colonel was too plainly fretting himself ill about it; he went pottering about forlornly—advertising, searching, and seeing people, but all of course to no purpose, and it told upon him. He was more like a man whose only son and heir had been stolen, than an Anglo-Indian officer who had lost a poodle. I had to affect the liveliest interest in all his inquiries and expeditions, and to listen to, and echo, the most extravagant eulogies of the departed, and the wear and tear of so much duplicity made me at last almost as ill as the Colonel himself.

I could not help seeing that Lilian was not nearly so much impressed by my elaborate concern as her relatives; and sometimes I detected an incredulous look in her frank brown eyes that made me very uneasy. Little by little, a rift widened between us, until at last in despair I determined to know the worst before the time came when it would be hopeless to speak at all. I chose a Sunday evening as we were walking across the green from church in the golden dusk, and then I ventured to speak to her of my love. She heard me to the end, and was evidently very much agitated. At last she murmured that it could not be, unless—no, it never could be now.

'Unless what?' I asked. 'Lilian—Miss Roseblade, something has come between us lately: you will tell me what that something is, won't you?'

'Do you want to know really?' she said, looking up at me through her tears. 'Then I'll tell you: it—it's Bingo!'

I started back overwhelmed. Did she know all? If not, how much did she suspect? I must find out that at once! 'What about Bingo?' I managed to pronounce, with a dry tongue.

'You never l-loved him when he was here,' she sobbed; 'you know you didn't!'

I was relieved to find it was no worse than this.

'No,' I said candidly; 'I did not love Bingo. Bingo didn't love me, Lilian; he was always looking out for a chance of nipping me somewhere. Surely you won't quarrel with me for that!'

'Not for that,' she said; 'only, why do you pretend to be so fond of him now, and so anxious to get him back again? Uncle John believes you, but I don't. I can see quite well that you wouldn't be glad to find him. You could find him easily if you wanted to!'

'What do you mean, Lilian?' I said hoarsely. 'How could I find him?' Again I feared the worst.

'You're in a Government office,' cried Lilian and if you only chose, you could easily g-get G-Government to find Bingo! What's the use of Government if it can't do that? Mr. Travers would have found him long ago if I'd asked him!'

Lilian had never been so childishly unreasonable as this before, and yet I loved her more madly than ever; but I did not like this allusion to Travers, a rising barrister, who lived with his sister in a pretty cottage near the station, and had shown symptoms of being attracted by Lilian.

He was away on circuit just then, luckily, but at least even he would have found it a hard task to find Bingo—there was comfort in that.

'You know that isn't just, Lilian,' I observed 'But only tell me what you want me to do?'

'Bub—bub—bring back Bingo!' she said.

'Bring back Bingo!' I cried in horror. 'But suppose I can't—suppose he's out of the country, or—dead, what then, Lilian?'

'I can't help it,' she said; 'but I don't believe he is out of the country or dead. And while I see you pretending to Uncle that you cared awfully about him, and going on doing nothing at all, it makes me think you're not quite—quite sincere! And I couldn't possibly marry any one while I thought that of him. And I shall always have that feeling unless you find Bingo!'

It was of no use to argue with her; I knew Lilian by that time. With her pretty caressing manner she united a latent obstinacy which it was hopeless to attempt to shake. I feared, too, that she was not quite certain as yet whether she cared for me or not, and that this condition of hers was an expedient to gain time.

I left her with a heavy heart. Unless I proved my worth by bringing back Bingo within a very short time, Travers would probably have everything his own way. And Bingo was dead!

However, I took heart. I thought that perhaps if I could succeed by my earnest efforts in persuading Lilian that I really was doing all in my power to recover the poodle, she might relent in time, and dispense with his actual production.

So, partly with this object, and partly to appease the remorse which now revived and stung me deeper than before, I undertook long and weary pilgrimages after office hours. I spent many pounds in advertisements; I interviewed dogs of every size, colour, and breed, and of course I took care to keep Lilian informed of each successive failure. But still her heart was not touched; she was firm. If I went on like that, she told me, I was certain to find Bingo one day—then, but not before, would her doubts be set at rest.

I was walking one day through the somewhat squalid district which lies between Bow Street and High Holborn, when I saw, in a small theatrical costumier's window, a handbill stating that a black poodle had 'followed a gentleman' on a certain date, and if not claimed and the finder remunerated before a stated time, would be sold to pay expenses.

I went in and got a copy of the bill to show Lilian, and although by that time I scarcely dared to look a poodle in the face, I thought I would go to the address given and see the animal, simply to be able to tell Lilian I had done so.

The gentleman whom the dog had very unaccountably followed was a certain Mr. William Blagg, who kept a little shop near Endell Street, and called himself a bird-fancier, though I should scarcely have credited him with the necessary imagination. He was an evil-browed ruffian in a fur cap, with a broad broken nose and little shifty red eyes, and after I had told him what I wanted, he took me through a horrible little den, stacked with piles of wooden, wire, and wicker prisons, each quivering with restless, twittering life, and then out into a back yard, in which were two or three rotten old kennels and tubs. 'That there's him,' he said, jerking his thumb to the farthest tub; 'follered me all the way 'ome from Kinsington Gardings, he did. Kim out, will yer?'

And out of the tub there crawled slowly, with a snuffling whimper and a rattling of its chain, the identical dog I had slain a few evenings before!

At least, so I thought for a moment, and felt as if I had seen a spectre; the resemblance was so exact—in size, in every detail, even to the little clumps of hair about the hind parts, even to the lop of half an ear, this dog might have been the 'doppel-gänger' of the deceased Bingo. I suppose, after all, one black poodle is very like any other black poodle of the same size, but the likeness startled me.

I think it was then that the idea occurred to me that here was a miraculous chance of securing the sweetest girl in the whole world, and at the same time atoning for my wrong by bringing back gladness with me to Shuturgarden. It only needed a little boldness; one last deception, and I could embrace truthfulness once more.

Almost unconsciously, when my guide turned round and asked,' Is that there dawg yourn?' I said hurriedly, 'Yes, yes—that's the dog I want, that—that's Bingo!'

'He don't seem to be a puttin' of 'isself out about seeing you again,' observed Mr. Blagg, as the poodle studied me with a calm interest.

'Oh, he's not exactly my dog, you see,' I said; 'he belongs to a friend of mine!'

He gave me a quick furtive glance. 'Then maybe you're mistook about him,' he said: 'and I can't run no risks. I was a goin' down in the country this 'ere werry evenin' to see a party as lives at Wistaria Willa,—he's been a hadwertisin' about a black poodle, he has!'

'But look here,' I said, 'that's me.'

He gave me a curious leer. 'No offence, you know, guv'nor,' he said, 'but I should wish for some evidence as to that afore I part with a vallyable dawg like this 'ere!'

'Well,' I said, 'here's one of my cards; will that do for you?'

He took it and spelt it out with a pretence of great caution, but I saw well enough that the old scoundrel suspected that if I had lost a dog at all, it was not this particular dog. 'Ah,' he said, as he put it in his pocket, 'if I part with him to you, I must be cleared of all risks. I can't afford to get into trouble about no mistakes. Unless you likes to leave him for a day or two, you must pay accordin', you see.'

I wanted to get the hateful business over as soon as possible. I did not care what I paid—Lilian was worth all the expense! I said I had no doubt myself as to the real ownership of the animal, but I would give him any sum in reason, and would remove the dog at once.

And so we settled it. I paid him an extortionate sum, and came away with a duplicate poodle, a canine counterfeit which I hoped to pass off at Shuturgarden as the long-lost Bingo.

I know it was wrong—it even came unpleasantly near dog-stealing—but I was a desperate man. I saw Lilian gradually slipping away from me, I knew that nothing short of this could ever recall her, I was sorely tempted, I had gone far on the same road already, it was the old story of being hung for a sheep. And so I fell.

Surely some who read this will be generous enough to consider the peculiar state of the case, and mingle a little pity with their contempt.

I was dining in town that evening and took my purchase home by a late train; his demeanour was grave and intensely respectable; he was not the animal to commit himself by any flagrant indiscretion—he was gentle and tractable, too, and in all respects an agreeable contrast in character to the original. Still, it may have been the after-dinner workings of conscience, but I could not help fancying that I saw a certain look in the creature's eyes, as if he were aware that he was required to connive at a fraud, and rather resented it.

If he would only be good enough to back me up! Fortunately, however, he was such a perfect facsimile of the outward Bingo, that the risk of detection was really inconsiderable.

When I got him home, I put Bingo's silver collar round his neck—congratulating myself on my forethought in preserving it, and took him in to see my mother. She accepted him as what he seemed, without the slightest misgiving; but this, though it encouraged me to go on, was not decisive, the spurious poodle would have to encounter the scrutiny of those who knew every tuft on the genuine animal's body!

Nothing would have induced me to undergo such an ordeal as that of personally restoring him to the Curries. We gave him supper, and tied him up on the lawn, where he howled dolefully all night, and buried bones.

The next morning I wrote a note to Mrs. Currie, expressing my pleasure at being able to restore the lost one, and another to Lilian, containing only the words, 'Will you believe now that I am sincere?' Then I tied both round the poodle's neck and dropped him over the wall into the Colonel's garden just before I started to catch my train to town.

I had an anxious walk home from the station that evening; I went round by the longer way, trembling the whole time lest I should meet any of the Currie household, to which I felt myself entirely unequal just then. I could not rest until I knew whether my fraud had succeeded, or if the poodle to which I had entrusted my fate had basely betrayed me; but my suspense was happily ended as soon as I entered my mother's room. 'You can't think how delighted those poor Curries were to see Bingo again,'she said at once; 'and they said such charming things about you, Algy—Lilian, particularly—quite affected she seemed, poor child! And they wanted you to go round and dine there and be thanked to-night, but at last I persuaded them to come to us instead. And they're going to bring the dog to make friends. Oh, and I met Frank Travers; he's back from circuit again now, so I asked him in too, to meet them!'

I drew a deep breath of relief. I had played a desperate game—but I had won! I could have wished, to be sure, that my mother had not thought of bringing in Travers on that of all evenings—but I hoped that I could defy him after this.

The Colonel and his people were the first to arrive; he and his wife being so effusively grateful that they made me very uncomfortable indeed; Lilian met me with downcast eyes, and the faintest possible blush, but she said nothing just then. Five minutes afterwards, when she and I were alone together in the conservatory, where I had brought her on pretence of showing a new begonia, she laid her hand on my sleeve and whispered, almost shyly, 'Mr. Weatherhead—Algernon! Can you ever forgive me for being so cruel and unjust to you?' And I replied that, upon the whole, I could.

We were not in that conservatory long, but, before we left it, beautiful Lilian Roseblade had consented to make my life happy. When we re-entered the drawing-room, we found Frank Travers, who had been told the story of the recovery, and I observed his jaw fall as he glanced at our faces, and noted the triumphant smile which I have no doubt mine wore, and the tender dreamy look in Lilian's soft eyes. Poor Travers, I was sorry for him, although I was not fond of him. Travers was a good type of the rising young Common Law barrister; tall, not bad-looking, with keen dark eyes, black whiskers, and the mobile forensic mouth, which can express every shade of feeling, from deferential assent to cynical incredulity; possessed, too, of an endless flow of conversation that was decidedly agreeable, if a trifle too laboriously so, he had been a dangerous rival. But all that was over now—he saw it himself at once, and during dinner sank into dismal silence, gazing pathetically at Lilian, and sighing almost obtrusively between the courses. His stream of small talk seemed to have been cut off at the main.

'You've done a kind thing, Weatherhead,' said the Colonel. 'I can't tell you all that dog is to me, and how I missed the poor beast. I'd quite given up all hope of ever seeing him again, and all the time there was Weatherhead, Mr. Travers, quietly searching all London till he found him! I shan't forget it. It shows a really kind feeling.'

I saw by Travers's face that he was telling himself he would have found fifty Bingos in half the time—if he had only thought of it; he smiled a melancholy assent to all the Colonel said, and then began to study me with an obviously depreciatory air.

'You can't think,' I heard Mrs. Currie telling my mother, 'how really touching it was to see poor dear Bingo's emotion at seeing all the old familiar objects again! He went up and sniffed at them all in turn, quite plainly recognising everything. And he was quite put out to find that we had moved his favourite ottoman out of the drawing-room. But he is so penitent, too, and so ashamed of having run away; he hardly dares to come when John calls him, and he kept under a chair in the hall all the morning—he wouldn't come in here either, so we had to leave him in your garden.'

'He's been sadly out of spirits all day,' said Lilian; 'he hasn't bitten one of the tradespeople.'

'Oh, he's all right, the rascal!' said the Colonel, cheerily; 'he'll be after the cats again as well as ever in a day or two.'

'Ah, those cats!' said my poor innocent mother. 'Algy, you haven't tried the air-gun on them again lately, have you? They're worse than ever.'

I troubled the Colonel to pass the claret; Travers laughed for the first time. 'That's a good idea,' he said, in that carrying 'bar-mess' voice of his; 'an air-gun for cats, ha, ha! Make good bags, eh, Weatherhead?' I said that I did, very good bags, and felt I was getting painfully red in the face.

'Oh, Algy is an excellent shot—quite a sportsman,' said my mother. 'I remember, oh, long ago, when we lived at Hammersmith, he had a pistol, and he used to strew crumbs in the garden for the sparrows, and shoot at them out of the pantry window; he frequently hit one.'

'Well,' said the Colonel, not much impressed by these sporting reminiscences, 'don't go rolling over our Bingo by mistake, you know, Weatherhead, my boy. Not but what you've a sort of right after this—only don't. I wouldn't go through it all twice for anything.'

'If you really won't take any more wine,' I said hurriedly, addressing the Colonel and Travers, 'suppose we all go out and have our coffee on the lawn? It—it will be cooler there.' For it was getting very hot indoors, I thought.

I left Travers to amuse the ladies—he could do no more harm now; and taking the Colonel aside, I seized the opportunity, as we strolled up and down the garden path, to ask his consent to Lilian's engagement to me. He gave it cordially. 'There's not a man in England,' he said, 'that I'd sooner see her married to after to-day. You're a quiet steady young fellow, and you've a good kind heart. As for the money, that's neither here nor there; Lilian won't come to you without a penny, you know. But really, my boy, you can hardly believe what it is to my poor wife and me to see that dog. Why, bless my soul, look at him now! What's the matter with him, eh?'

To my unutterable horror I saw that that miserable poodle, after begging unnoticed at the tea-table for some time, had retired to an open space before it, where he was now industriously standing on his head.

We gathered round and examined the animal curiously, as he continued to balance himself gravely in his abnormal position. 'Good gracious, John,' cried Mrs. Currie, 'I never saw Bingo do such a thing before in his life!'

'Very odd,' said the Colonel, putting up his glasses; 'never learnt that from me.'

'I tell you what I fancy it is,' I suggested wildly. 'You see, he was always a sensitive, excitable animal, and perhaps the—the sudden joy of his return has gone to his head—upset him, you know.'

They seemed disposed to accept this solution, and indeed I believe they would have credited Bingo with every conceivable degree of sensibility; but I felt myself that if this unhappy animal had many more of these accomplishments I was undone, for the original Bingo had never been a dog of parts.

'It's very odd,' said Travers, reflectively, as the dog recovered his proper level, 'but I always thought that it was half the right ear that Bingo had lost?'

'So it is, isn't it?' said the Colonel. 'Left, eh? Well, I thought myself it was the right.'

My heart almost stopped with terror—I had altogether forgotten that. I hastened to set the point at rest. 'Oh, it was the left,' I said positively; 'I know it because I remember so particularly thinking how odd it was that it should be the left ear, and not the right!' I told myself this should be positively my last lie.

'Why odd?' asked Frank Travers, with his most offensive Socratic manner.

'My dear fellow, I can't tell you,' I said impatiently; 'everything seems odd when you come to think at all about it.'

'Algernon,' said Lilian later on, 'will you tell Aunt Mary and Mr. Travers, and—and me, how it was you came to find Bingo? Mr. Travers is quite anxious to hear all about it.'

I could not very well refuse; I sat down and told the story, all my own way. I painted Blagg, perhaps, rather bigger and blacker than life, and described an exciting scene, in which I recognised Bingo by his collar in the streets, and claimed and bore him off then and there in spite of all opposition.

I had the inexpressible pleasure of seeing Travers grinding his teeth with envy as I went on, and feeling Lilian's soft, slender hand glide silently into mine as I told my tale in the twilight.

All at once, just as I reached the climax, we heard the poodle barking furiously at the hedge which separated my garden from the road. 'There's a foreign-looking man staring over the hedge,' said Lilian; 'Bingo always did hate foreigners.'

There certainly was a swarthy man there, and, though I had no reason for it then, somehow my heart died within me at the sight of him.

'Don't be alarmed, sir,' cried the Colonel, 'the dog won't bite you—unless there's a hole in the hedge anywhere.'

The stranger took off his small straw hat with a sweep. 'Ah, I am not afraid,' he said, and his accent proclaimed him a Frenchman, 'he is not enrage at me. May I ask, is it pairmeet to speak wiz Misterre Vezzered?'

I felt I must deal with this person alone, for I feared the worst; and, asking them to excuse me, I went to the hedge and faced the Frenchman with the frightful calm of despair. He was a short, stout little man, with blue cheeks, sparkling black eyes, and a vivacious walnut-coloured countenance; he wore a short black alpaca coat, and a large white cravat with an immense oval malachite brooch in the centre of it, which I mention because I found myself staring mechanically at it during the interview.

'My name is Weatherhead,' I began, with the bearing of a detected pickpocket. 'Can I be of any service to you?'

'Of a great service,' he said emphatically; 'you can restore to me ze poodle vich I see zere!'

Nemesis had called at last in the shape of a rival claimant. I staggered for an instant; then I said, 'Oh, I think you are under a mistake—that dog is not mine.'

'I know it,' he said; 'zere 'as been leetle mistake, so if ze dog is not to you, you give him back to me, hein?'

'I tell you,' I said, 'that poodle belongs to the gentleman over there.' And I pointed to the Colonel, seeing that it was best now to bring him into the affair without delay.

'You are wrong,' he said doggedly; 'ze poodle is my poodle! And I was direct to you—it is your name on ze carte!' And he presented me with that fatal card which I had been foolish enough to give to Blagg as a proof of my identity. I saw it all now; the old villain had betrayed me, and to earn a double reward had put the real owner on my track.

I decided to call the Colonel at once, and attempt to brazen it out with the help of his sincere belief in the dog.

'Eh, what's that; what's it all about?' said the Colonel, bustling up, followed at intervals by the others.

The Frenchman raised his hat again. 'I do not vant to make a trouble,' he began, 'but zere is leetle mistake. My word of honour, sare, I see my own poodle in your garden. Ven I appeal to zis gentilman to restore 'im he reffer me to you.'

'You must allow me to know my own dog, sir,' said the Colonel. 'Why, I've had him from a pup. Bingo, old boy, you know your master, don't you?'

But the brute ignored him altogether, and began to leap wildly at the hedge, in frantic efforts to join the Frenchman. It needed no Solomon to decide his ownership!

'I tell you, you 'ave got ze wrong poodle—it is my own dog, my Azor! He remember me well, you see? I lose him it is three, four days.... I see a nottice zat he is found, and ven I go to ze address zey tell me, "Oh, he is reclaim, he is gone wiz a strangaire who has advertise." Zey show me ze placard, I follow 'ere, and ven I arrive, I see my poodle in ze garden before me!'

'But look here,' said the Colonel, impatiently; 'it's all very well to say that, but how can you prove it? I give you my word that the dog belongs to me! You must prove your claim, eh, Travers?'

'Yes,' said Travers, judicially, 'mere assertion is no proof: it's oath against oath, at present.'

'Attend an instant—your poodle was he 'ighly train, had he some talents—a dog viz tricks, eh?'

'No, he's not,' said the Colonel; 'I don't like to see dogs taught to play the fool—there's none of that nonsense about him, sir!'

'Ah, remark him well, then. Azor, mon chou, danse donc un peu!'

And on the foreigner's whistling a lively air, that infernal poodle rose on his hind legs and danced solemnly about half-way round the garden! We inside followed his movements with dismay. 'Why, dash it all!' cried the disgusted Colonel, 'he's dancing along like a damned mountebank! But it's my Bingo for all that!'

'You are not convince? You shall see more. Azor, ici! Pour Beesmarck, Azor!' (the poodle barked ferociously). 'Pour Gambetta!' (he wagged his tail and began to leap with joy). 'Meurs pour la Patrie!'— and the too-accomplished animal rolled over as if killed in battle!

'Where could Bingo have picked up so much French!' cried Lilian, incredulously.

'Or so much French history?' added that serpent Travers.

'Shall I command 'im to jomp, or reverse 'imself?' inquired the obliging Frenchman.

'We've seen that, thank you,' said the Colonel, gloomily. 'Upon my word, I don't know what to think. It can't be that that's not my Bingo after all—I'll never believe it!'

I tried a last desperate stroke. 'Will you come round to the front?' I said to the Frenchman; 'I'll let you in, and we can discuss the matter quietly.' Then, as we walked back together, I asked him eagerly what he would take to abandon his claims and let the Colonel think the poodle was his after all.

He was furious—he considered himself insulted; with great emotion he informed me that the dog was the pride of his life (it seems to be the mission of black poodles to serve as domestic comforts of this priceless kind!), that he would not part with him for twice his weight in gold.

'Figure,' he began, as we joined the others, 'zat zis gentilman 'ere 'as offer me money for ze dog! He agrees zat it is to me, you see? Ver well zen, zere is no more to be said!'

'Why, Weatherhead, have you lost faith too, then?' said the Colonel.

I saw that it was no good—all I wanted now was to get out of it creditably and get rid of the Frenchman. 'I'm sorry to say,' I replied, 'that I'm afraid I've been deceived by the extraordinary likeness. I don't think, on reflection, that that is Bingo!'

'What do you think, Travers?' asked the Colonel.

'Well, since you ask me,' said Travers, with quite unnecessary dryness, 'I never did think so.'

'Nor I,' said the Colonel; 'I thought from the first that was never my Bingo. Why, Bingo would make two of that beast!'

And Lilian and her aunt both protested that they had had their doubts from the first.

'Zen you pairmeet zat I remove 'im?' said the Frenchman.

'Certainly' said the Colonel; and after some apologies on our part for the mistake, he went off in triumph, with the detestable poodle frisking after him.

When he had gone the Colonel laid his hand kindly on my shoulder. 'Don't look so cut up about it, my boy,' he said; 'you did your best—there was a sort of likeness, to any one who didn't know Bingo as we did.'

Just then the Frenchman again appeared at the hedge. 'A thousand pardons,' he said, 'but I find zis upon my dog—it is not to me. Suffer me to restore it viz many compliments.'

It was Bingo's collar. Travers took it from his hand and brought it to us.

'This was on the dog when you stopped that fellow, didn't you say?' he asked me.

One more lie—and I was so-weary of falsehood! 'Y-yes,' I said reluctantly, that was so.'

'Very extraordinary,' said Travers; 'that's the wrong poodle beyond a doubt, but when he's found, he's wearing the right dog's collar! Now how do you account for that?'

'My good fellow,' I said impatiently, 'I'm not in the witness-box. I can't account for it. It—it's a mere coincidence!'

'But look here, my dear Weatherhead,' argued Travers (whether in good faith or not I never could quite make out), 'don't you see what a tremendously important link it is? Here's a dog who (as I understand the facts) had a silver collar, with his name engraved on it, round his neck at the time he was lost. Here's that identical collar turning up soon afterwards round the neck of a totally different dog! We must follow this up; we must get at the bottom of it somehow! With a clue like this, we're sure to find out, either the dog himself, or what's become of him! Just try to recollect exactly what happened, there's a good fellow. This is just the sort of thing I like!'

It was the sort of thing I did not enjoy at all. 'You must excuse me to-night, Travers,' I said uncomfortably; 'you see, just now it's rather a sore subject for me—and I'm not feeling very well!' I was grateful just then for a reassuring glance of pity and confidence from Lilian's sweet eyes which revived my drooping spirits for the moment.

'Yes, we'll go into it to-morrow, Travers,' said the Colonel; 'and then—hullo, why, there's that confounded Frenchman again!'

It was indeed; he came prancing back delicately, with a malicious enjoyment on his wrinkled face. 'Once more I return to apologise,' he said. 'My poodle 'as permit 'imself ze grave indiscretion to make a very big 'ole at ze bottom of ze garden!'

I assured him that it was of no consequence. 'Perhaps,' he replied, looking steadily at me through his keen half-shut eyes, 'you vill not say zat ven you regard ze 'ole. And you others, I spik to you: somtimes von loses a somzing vich is qvite near all ze time. It is ver droll, eh? my vord, ha, ha, ha!' And he ambled off, with an aggressively fiendish laugh that chilled my blood.

'What the dooce did he mean by that, eh?' said the Colonel, blankly.

'Don't know,' said Travers; 'suppose we go and inspect the hole?'

But before that I had contrived to draw near it myself, in deadly fear lest the Frenchman's last words had contained some innuendo which I had not understood.

It was light enough still for me to see something, at the unexpected horror of which I very nearly fainted.

That thrice accursed poodle which I had been insane enough to attempt to foist upon the Colonel must, it seems, have buried his supper the night before very near the spot in which I had laid Bingo, and in his attempts to exhume his bone had brought the remains of my victim to the surface!

There the corpse lay, on the very top of the excavations. Time had not, of course, improved its appearance, which was ghastly in the extreme, but still plainly recognisable by the eye of affection.

'It's a very ordinary hole,' I gasped, putting myself before it and trying to turn them back. 'Nothing in it—nothing at all!'

'Except one Algernon Weatherhead, Esq., eh?' whispered Travers jocosely in my ear.

'No, but,' persisted the Colonel, advancing, 'look here! Has the dog damaged any of your shrubs?'

'No, no!' I cried piteously, 'quite the reverse. Let's all go indoors now; it's getting so cold!'

'See, there is a shrub or something uprooted!' said the Colonel, still coming nearer that fatal hole. 'Why, hullo, look there! What's that?'

Lilian, who was by his side, gave a slight scream. 'Uncle,' she cried, 'it looks like—like Bingo!'

The Colonel turned suddenly upon me. 'Do you hear?' he demanded, in a choked voice. 'You hear what she says? Can't you speak out? Is that our Bingo?'

I gave it up at last; I only longed to be allowed to crawl away under something! 'Yes,' I said in a dull whisper, as I sat down heavily on a garden seat, 'yes ... that's Bingo ... misfortune ... shoot him ... quite an accident!'

There was a terrible explosion after that; they saw at last how I had deceived them, and put the very worst construction upon everything. Even now I writhe impotently at times, and my cheeks smart and tingle with humiliation, as I recall that scene—the Colonel's very plain speaking, Lilian's passionate reproaches and contempt, and her aunt's speechless prostration of disappointment.

I made no attempt to defend myself; I was not perhaps the complete villain they deemed me, but I felt dully that no doubt it all served me perfectly right.

Still I do not think I am under any obligation to put their remarks down in black and white here.

Travers had vanished at the first opportunity—whether out of delicacy, or the fear of breaking out into unseasonable mirth, I cannot say; and shortly afterwards the others came to where I sat silent with bowed head, and bade me a stern and final farewell.

And then, as the last gleam of Lilian's white dress vanished down the garden path, I laid my head down on the table amongst the coffee-cups and cried like a beaten child.

I got leave as soon as I could and went abroad. The morning after my return I noticed, while shaving, that there was a small square marble tablet placed against the wall of the Colonel's garden. I got my opera-glass and read—and pleasant reading it was—the following inscription:—

IN AFFECTIONATE MEMORY OF B I N G O, SECRETLY AND CRUELLY PUT TO DEATH, IN COLD BLOOD; BY A NEIGHBOUR AND FRIEND. JUNE, 1881

If this explanation of mine ever reaches my neighbours' eyes, I humbly hope they will have the humanity either to take away or tone down that tablet. They cannot conceive what I suffer, when curious visitors insist, as they do every day, in spelling out the words from our windows, and asking me countless questions about them!

Sometimes I meet the Curries about the village, and, as they pass me with averted heads, I feel myself growing crimson. Travers is almost always with Lilian now. He has given her a dog—a fox-terrier—and they take ostentatiously elaborate precautions to keep it out of my garden.

I should like to assure them here that they need not be under any alarm. I have shot one dog.


## THE STORY OF A SUGAR PRINCE

Of course he may have been really a fairy prince, and I should be sorry to contradict any one who chose to say so. For he was only about three inches high, he had rose-pink cheeks and bright yellow curling locks, he wore a doublet and hose which fitted him perfectly, and a little cap and feather, all of delicately contrasted shades of blue—and this does seem a fair description of a fairy prince.

But then he was painted—very cleverly—but still only painted, on a slab of prepared sugar, and his back was a plain white blank; while the regular fairies all have more than one side to them, and I am obliged to say that I never before happened to come across a real fairy prince who was nothing but paint and sugar.

For all that he may, as I said before, have been a fairy prince, and whether he was or not does not matter in the least—for he at any rate quite believed he was one.

As yet there had been very little romance or enchantment in his life, which, as far as he could remember, had all been spent in a long shop, full of sweet and subtle scents, where the walls were lined with looking-glass and fitted with shelves on which stood rows of glass jars, containing pastilles and jujubes of every colour, shape, and flavour in the world—a shop where, in summer, a strange machine for making cooling drinks gurgled and sputtered all day long, and in winter, the large plate-glass windows were filled with boxes made of painted silk from Paris, so charmingly expensive and useless that rich people bought them eagerly to give to one another.

The prince generally lay on one of the counters between two beds of sugar roses and violets in a glass case, on either side of which stood a figure of highly coloured plaster.

One was a major of some unknown regiment; he had an immense head, with goggling eyes and a very red complexion, and this head would unscrew so that he could be filled with comfits, which, though it hurt him fearfully every time this was done, he was proud of, because it always astonished people.

The other figure was an old brown gipsy woman in a red cloak and a striped petticoat, with a head which, although it wouldn't take off, was always nodding and grinning mysteriously from morning to night.

It was to her that the prince (for we shall have to call him 'the prince,' as I don't know his other name—if he ever had one) owed all his notions of Fairyland and his high birth.

'You let the old gipsy alone for knowing a prince when she sees one,' she would say, nodding at him with encouragement. 'They've kept you out of your rights all this time; but wait a while, and see if one of these clumsy giants that are always bustling in and out doesn't help you; you'll be restored to your kingdom, never fear!'

But the major used to get angry at her prophecies: 'It's all nonsense,' he used to say, 'the boy's no more a prince than I am, and he'll never be noticed by anybody, unless he learns to unscrew his head and hold comfits—like a soldier and a gentleman!'

However, the prince believed the gipsy, and every morning, as the shutters were taken down, and grey mist, brilliant sunshine, or brown fog stole into the close shop, he wondered whether the day had come which would see his restoration to his kingdom.

And at last the day really came; some one who had been buying sugar violets and roses noticed the prince in the middle of them and bought him too, to his immense delight. 'What did the old gipsy tell you, eh?' said the old woman, wagging her head wisely; 'you see, it has all come true!'

Even the major was convinced now, for, before the prince had been packed up, he whispered to him that if at any time he wanted a commander-in-chief, why, he knew where to send for him. 'Yes, I will remember,' said the prince; 'and you,' he added to the gipsy, 'you shall be my prime minister!'—for he was so ignorant of politics that he actually thought an old woman could be prime minister.

And then, before he could finish saying good-bye and hearing their congratulations, he was covered with several wrappers of white paper and plunged into complete darkness, which he did not mind at all, he was so happy.

After that he remembered no more until he was unwrapped and placed upright on the top of a dazzling white dome which stood in the very centre of a long plain, where a host of the strangest forms were scattered about in bewildering confusion.

On each side of him tall twisted trunks of sparkling glass and silver sprang high into the air, and from their tops the cool green branches swayed gently down, while round their bases velvet-petalled flowers bloomed in a bed of soft moss.

Farther away, an exquisite temple, made of a sort of delicate gold-coloured crystal, rose out of the crowd of gorgeous things that surrounded it, and this crowd, as the prince's eyes became accustomed to the splendour, gradually separated itself into various forms of loveliness.

He saw high curiously moulded masses of transparent amber, within which ruby and emerald gems glowed dimly; mounds of rose-flushed snow, and blocks of creamy marble; and in the space between these were huge platforms of silver and porcelain, on which were piled heaps of treasures that he knew must be priceless, though he could not guess what they were all used for.

But amidst all these were certain grim shapes; some seemed to be the carcases of fearful beasts, whose heads had all been struck off, but who had evidently shown such courage in death that they had earned the respect of the brave hunters who had vanquished them—for rosettes had been pinned on their rough breasts, and their stiffened limbs were bound together by bright-hued ribbons.

Then there was one monstrous head of some brute larger still, which could not have been quite killed even then, for its tawny eyes were still glaring with fury—the prince could easily have stood upright between its grinning jaws if he had wanted to do so; but he had no intention of doing any such thing, for though he was quite as brave as most fairy princes he was not foolhardy.

And there were big enchanted castles with no doors nor windows in them, and inhabited by restless monsters—dragons most likely—who had thrust their scaly black claws through the roofs.

Perhaps he was a little frightened by some of the ugliest shapes at first, but he soon grew used to them, and had no room for any other feelings than pride and joy. For this was Fairyland at last, stranger and more beautiful than anything he could have dreamed of—he had come into his kingdom!

He was going to live in that lacework palace; those dragons would come fawning out of their lairs presently, and do homage to him; these formidable dead creatures had been slain to do him honour; and he was the rightful owner of all these treasures of gold, and silk, and gems.

He must not forget, he thought, that he owed it all to the good-natured giants who had brought him here: no, when they came in—as of course they would—to pay their respects, he would thank them graciously and reward them liberally out of his new wealth.

There was a silver giraffe, stiff and old-fashioned, under a palm-tree hard by, which must have guessed from the prince's proud gay smile that he was deceiving himself and had no idea of his real position.

But the giraffe did not make any attempt to warn him, either because it had seen so many things all round it consumed in its day that the selfish fear that it too would be cut up and handed round some evening kept it preoccupied and silent, or else because, being only electro-plated and hollow inside, it had no feelings of any kind.

By-and-by the doors opened, and delicious bursts of music floated into the room, mingled with scraps of conversation and ripples of fresh laughter; servants came noiselessly in and increased the glare of a kind of sun that hung above the plain, and a host of smaller lights suddenly started up and shone softly through shades of silk and paper.

The music stopped, the laughter and voices grew louder and came nearer, there was the sound of approaching feet—and then a whole army of mortals surrounded the prince's kingdom.

They were a far smaller and finer race than the giants he had seen hitherto, with pretty fresh complexions, and wearing, some of them, soft shimmering dresses that he thought only fairies ever wore. After a little confusion, they ranged themselves in one long line completely round the plain; the taller beings glided softly about behind, and the prince prepared himself to receive their congratulations with proper dignity and modesty.

But these giants certainly had very odd ways of showing their loyalty, for they saluted him with a clinking and clattering so deafening that they would have drowned the noise of a million gnomes forging fairy armour, while every now and then came a loud report, after which a golden sparkling cascade fell creaming and bubbling from somewhere above into the crystal reservoirs prepared for it.

It was all very gratifying, no doubt—and yet, though they all pretended to be honouring him, no one seemed to pay him any more particular attention; he thought perhaps they might be feeling abashed in his presence, and that he must manage to reassure them.

But while he was thinking how he could best do this, he began to be aware that along the whole of that glittering plain things were being done without his permission which were scandalous and insulting—he saw the grisly carcases cut swiftly into pieces with flashing blades, or torn limb from limb deliberately; all the dragons were attacked and overpowered, and hauled out unresisting from their strongholds; even the fierce head was gashed hideously behind the ears!

He tried to speak and ask them what they meant by such audacity, but he could not make them hear as he could the major and the old gipsy; so he was obliged to look on while one by one the trophies dedicated to his glory were changed to shapeless heaps of ruin.

And, unless he was mistaken, the greater part of them were actually disappearing from sight altogether! It seemed impossible, for where could they all go to? and yet nothing now remained of the huge carcases but a meagre framework of bone, hanging together by shreds of skin; the strong castles were roofless walls with gaping breaches in them; and could it be that the more attractive objects were beginning to melt away in the same mysterious manner? Was it enchantment, or how—how on earth did they manage to do it?

He was no happier when he found out—for though, of course, to us eating is quite an ordinary everyday affair, only think what a shock the first sight of it must have been to a delicate fairy prince, whose mouth was simply a cherry-coloured curve, and not made to open on any terms!

He saw all the treasures he had looked upon as his very own being lifted to a long line of mouths of all sizes and shapes; the mouths opened to various widths, and—the treasures vanished, he could not tell how or where.

The mellow amber tottered and quivered for a while and was gone; even the solid creamy marble was hacked in pieces and absorbed; nothing, however beautiful or fantastic, escaped instant annihilation between those terrible bars of scarlet and flashing ivory.

Could this be Fairyland, this plain where all things beautiful were doomed—or had they brought him back to his kingdom only to make this cruel fun of him, and destroy his riches one by one before his eyes?

But before he could find any answers to these sad questions he chanced to look straight in front of him, and there he saw a face which made his little sugar heart almost melt within him, with a curious feeling, half pleasure, half pain, that was quite new to him.

It was a girl's face, of course, and the prince had not looked at her very long before he forgot all about his kingdom.

He was relieved to see that she at least was too generous to join in the work of destruction that was going on all around her—indeed, she seemed to dislike it as much as he did himself, for only a little of the tinted snow passed her soft lips.

Now and then she laughed a little silvery laugh, and shook out her rippling gold-brown hair at something the being next to her said—a great boy-mortal, with a red face, bold eyes, and grasping brown hands, which were fatal to everything within their range.

How the prince did hate that boy!—he found to his joy that he could understand what they said, and began to listen jealously to their conversation.

'I say,' the boy (whose name, it seemed, was Bertie) was saying, as he received a plateful of floating fragments of the lacework palace, 'you aren't eating anything, Mabel. Don't you care about suppers? I do.'

'I'm not hungry,' she said, evidently feeling this a distinction; 'I've been out so much this fortnight.'

'How jolly!' he observed, 'I only wish I had. But I say,' he added confidentially, 'won't they make you take a grey powder soon? They would me.'

'I'm never made to take anything at all nasty,' she said—and the prince was indignant that any one should have dared to think otherwise.

'I suppose,' continued the boy, 'you didn't manage to get any of that cake the conjurer made in Uncle John's hat, did you?'

'No, indeed,' she said, and made a little face; 'I don't think I should like cake that came out of anybody's hat!'

'It was very decent cake,' he said; 'I got a lot of it. I was afraid it might spoil my appetite for supper—but it hasn't.'

'What a very greedy boy you are, Bertie,' she remarked; 'I suppose you could eat anything?'

'At home I think I could, pretty nearly,' he said, with a proud confidence, 'but not at old Tokoe's, I can't. Tokoe's is where I go to school, you know. I can't stand the resurrection-pie on Saturdays—all the week they save up the bones and rags and things, and when it comes up—'

'I don't want to hear,' she interrupted; 'you talk about nothing but horrid things to eat, and it isn't a bit interesting.'

Bertie allowed himself a brief interval for refreshment unalloyed by conversation, after which he began again: 'Mabel, if they have dancing after supper, dance with me.'

'Are you sure you know how to dance?' she inquired rather fastidiously.

'Oh, I can get through all right,' he replied. 'I've learnt. It's not harder than drilling. I can dance the Highland Schottische and the Swedish dance, any-way.'

'Any one can dance those. I don't call that dancing,' she said.

'Well, but try me once, Mabel; say you will,' said he.

'I don't believe they will have dancing,' she said; 'there are so many very young children here and they get in the way so. But I hope there won't be any more games—games are stupid.'

'Only to girls,' said Bertie; 'girls never care about any fun.'

'Not your kind of fun,' she said, a little vaguely. 'I don't mind hide-and-seek in a nice old house with long passages and dark corners and secret panels—and ghosts even—that's jolly; but I don't care much about running round and round a row of silly chairs, trying to sit down when the music stops and keep other people out—I call it rude.'

'You didn't seem to think it so rude just now,' he retorted; 'you were laughing quite as much as any one; and I saw you push young Bobby Meekin off the last chair of all, and sit on it yourself, anyhow.'

'Bertie, you didn't,' she cried, flushing angrily.

'I did though.'

'But I tell you I didn't!'

'And I say you did!'

'If you will go on saying I did, when I'm quite sure I never did anything of the sort,' she said, 'please don't speak to me again; I shan't answer if you do. And I think you're a particularly ill-bred boy—not polite, like my brothers.'

'Your brothers are every bit as rude as I am. If they aren't, they're milksops—I should be sorry to be a milksop.'

'My brothers are not milksops—they could fight you!' she cried, with a little defiant ring in her voice that the prince thought perfectly charming.

'As if a girl knew anything about fighting,' said Bertie; 'why, I could fight your brothers all stuck in a row!'

'That you couldn't,' from Mabel, and 'I could then, so now!' from Bertie, until at last Mabel refused to answer any more of Bertie's taunts, as they grew decidedly offensive; and, finding that she took refuge in disdainful silence, he consumed tart after tart with gloomy determination.

And then all at once, Mabel, having nothing to do, chanced to look across to the white dome on which the prince was standing, and she opened her beautiful grey eyes with a pleased surprise as she saw him.

All this time the prince had been falling deeper and deeper in love with her; at first he had felt almost certain that she was a princess and his destined bride; he was rather small for her, certainly, though he did not know how very much smaller he was; but Fairyland, he had always been told, was full of resources—he could easily be filled out to her size, or, better still, she might be brought down to his.

But he had begun to give up these wild fancies already, and even to fear that she would go away without having once noticed him; and now she was looking at him as if she found him pleasant to look at, as if she would like to know him.

At last, evidently after some struggle, she turned to the offending Bertie, and spoke his name softly; but Bertie could not give up the luxury of sulking with her all at once, and so he looked another way.

'Is it Pax, Bertie?' she asked. (She had not had brothers for nothing.)

'No, it isn't,' said Bertie.

'Oh, you want to sulk? I thought only girls sulked,' she said; 'but it doesn't matter, I only wanted to tell you something.'

His curiosity was too much for his dignity. 'Well—what?' he asked, gruffly enough.

'Only,' she said, 'that I've been thinking over things, and I dare say you could fight my brothers—only not all together and I'm not sure that Charlie wouldn't beat you.'

'Charlie! I could settle him in five minutes,' muttered Bertie, only half appeased.

'Oh, not in five, Bertie,' cried Mabel, 'ten, perhaps; but you'd never want to, would you, when he's my brother? And now,' she added, 'we're friends again, aren't we, Bertie?'

He was a cynic in his way—'I see,' he said, 'you want something out of me; you should have thought of that before you quarrelled, you know!'

Mabel contracted her eyebrows and bit her lip for a moment, then she said meekly—

'I know I should, Bertie; but I thought perhaps you wouldn't mind doing this for me. I can ask the boy on my other side—he's a stupid-looking boy, and I don't care about knowing him—still, if you won't do it—'

'Oh, well, I don't mind,' he said, softened at once. 'What is it you want?'

'Bertie,' she whispered breathlessly, 'you'll be quite a nice boy if you'll only get me that dear little sugar prince off the cake there; you can reach him better than I can, and—and I don't quite like to—only, be quick, or some one else will get him first.'

And in another second the enraptured prince found himself lying on her plate!

'Isn't he lovely?' she cried.

'Not bad,' said Bertie; 'give us a bit—I got him for you, you know.'

'Give you a bit!' she cried, with the keenest horror and disgust. 'Bertie! you don't really think I wanted him to—to eat.'

'Oh, the paint doesn't matter,' he said; 'I've eaten lots of them.'

'You really are too horrid,' she said; 'all you think about is eating things. I can't bear greedy boys. I won't have anything to do with you any more; after this we'll be perfect strangers.'

He stared helplessly at her; he had made friends and done all she asked of him, and, just because he begged for a share in the spoil, she had treated him like this! It was too bad of her—it served him right for bothering about a girl.

He would have told her what he thought about it, only just then there was a general rising. The prince was carried tenderly upstairs, entrusted with many cautions to a trim maid, and laid to rest wrapped in a soft lace handkerchief upon a dressing-table, to dream of the new life in store for him to the accompaniment of faintly heard music and laughter from below.

He had given up all his old ideas of recovering his kingdom and marrying a princess—very likely he might not be a fairy prince after all, and he felt now that he did not very much care if he wasn't.

He was going to be Mabel's for evermore, and that was worth all Fairyland to him. How bewitching her anger had been when Bertie suspected her of wanting the prince for her own eating. (The prince had already found out that eating meant the way in which these ruthless mortals made everything beautiful pass away between their sharp teeth.)

She had pitied and protected him; might she not some day come to love him? If he had only known what a little sugar fool he was making of himself, I think he would certainly have dissolved into syrup for very shame.

Mabel came up to fetch him at last; they had fastened something white and fleecy round her head and shoulders, and her face was flushed and her eyes seemed a darker grey as she took him out of the handkerchief, with a cry of delight at finding him quite safe, and hurried downstairs with him.

While she was waiting in the hall for her carriage, the prince heard the last of Bertie; he came up to her and whispered spitefully, 'Well, you've kept your word, you've not looked at me since supper, all because I thought you meant to eat that sugar thing off the cake! Now I just tell you this—you needn't pretend you don't like sweets—I wouldn't give much for that figure's lasting a week, now!'

She only glanced at him with calm disdain, and passed on under the awning to her carriage, where her brothers were waiting for her, and Bertie was left with a recollection that would make his first fortnight under old Tokoe's roof even bitterer than usual to him.

What a deliciously dreamy drive home that was for the prince; he lay couched on Mabel's soft palm, thinking how cool and satiny it was, and how different from the hot coarse hands which had touched him hitherto.

She said nothing to her brothers, who were curled up, grey indistinct forms, opposite; she sat quietly at the side of the servant who had come to fetch them, and now and then in the faint light the prince could see her smiling with half-shut sleepy eyes at some pleasant recollection.

If that drive could only have gone on for ever! but it came to an end soon, very soon.

A little later his tired little protectress placed him where she could see him when first she awoke the next day, and all that night the prince stood on guard upon the high mantelpiece in the night nursery, thinking of the kiss, half-childish and half-playful, she had given him just before she left him at his post.

The next morning Mabel woke up tired, and, if it must be confessed, a little cross; but the prince thought she looked lovelier than even on the night before, in her plain dark dress and fresh white pinafore and crossbands.

She took him down with her to breakfast, and stationed him near her plate—and then he made a discovery.

She, too, could make the solid things around her vanish in the very way of which he thought she disapproved so strongly!

It was done, as she seemed to do everything, very daintily and prettily—but still the things did disappear, somehow, and it was a shock.

She called the attention of her governess—who was a pale lady, with a very prominent forehead and round spectacles—to the prince's good looks, and the governess admitted that he was pretty, but cautioned Mabel not to eat him, as these highly-coloured confections invariably contained deleterious matter, and were therefore unwholesome.

'Oh,' said Mabel, defending her favourite with great animation, 'but not this one, Miss Pringle. Because I heard Mrs. Goodchild tell somebody last night that she was always so careful to get only sweets painted with "pure vegetable colours," she called it. But that wouldn't matter—for of course I shall never want to eat this little man!'

'Oh, of course not,' said the governess, with a smile that struck the prince as being unpleasant—though he did not know exactly why, and he was glad to forget it in watching the play of Mabel's pretty restless fingers on the table-cloth.

By-and-by the nurse came in, carrying something which he had never seen anything at all like before, and which frightened him very much. It was called as he soon found, a 'Baby,' and it goggled round it with glassy, meaningless eyes, and clucked fearfully somewhere deep down in its throat, while it stretched out feeble little wrinkled hands, exactly like yellow starfish.

'There, there, then!' said the nurse (which seems to be the right thing to say to a baby). 'See, Miss Mabel, he's asking for that to play with.'

Now that happened to be the sugar prince.

Mabel seemed completely in the power of this monster, for she dared not refuse it anything; she crossed almost timidly to it now, and laid the prince in one of its starfish, only entreating that nurse would not allow it to put him in its mouth.

But the baby did not try to do this; its vacant countenance only creased into an idiotic grin, as it began to take a great deal of notice of him; and its way of taking notice was to shake the prince violently up and down, till he was quite giddy.

After doing this several times, it ducked him quite suddenly down, head-foremost, into the nearest cup of tea.

The poor prince felt as if he were all softening and crumbling away into nothing, but it was only some of the paint coming off; and before he could be ducked a second time, Mabel, with a cry of dismay, rescued him from the indignant baby, which howled in a dreadful manner.

She dried him tenderly on her handkerchief, and then, as she saw the result, suddenly began to weep inconsolably herself. 'Oh, see what Baby's done!' she gasped between her sobs; 'all his lovely complexion ruined, spoilt ... I wish somebody would just spoil Baby's face for him, and see how he likes it.... If he isn't slapped at once—I'll never love him again!'

But nobody slapped the baby—it was soothed; and, besides, all the slaps hand could bestow would not bring back the prince's lost beauty.

His face was all the colours of the rainbow now; the yellow of his curls had run into his forehead, his brown eyes were smudged across his nose, and his cherry lips smeared upon his cheeks, while all the blue of his doublet had spread up to his chin.

He knew from what they were all saying that this had happened to him, but he did not mind it much, except at first; he had never been vain of his beauty, and it was delightful to hear Mabel's little tender laments over his misfortune; so long as she cared for him as he was—what did anything else matter?

In the schoolroom that morning he leaned against her writing-desk, and watched her turning fat books lazily over and inking her fair little hands, until she shut them all up with an impatient bang and yawned.

Why was it that at that precise moment the prince began to feel uncomfortable?

'Is it near dinner-time, Miss Pringle?' she asked. 'I'm so awfully hungry!'

The governess's watch showed an hour more to wait.

'I wonder if Comfitt would give me some cake if I ran down and asked her!' said Mabel next.

The governess thought Mabel had much better wait patiently till dinner-time without spoiling her appetite.

'Oh, very well,' said Mabel; 'what a bore it is to be hungry too soon, isn't it?'

Then she took the faded prince up and looked at him mournfully. 'What a shame of Baby!' she said; 'I wanted to keep him always to look at—but I don't see how I can very well now, do you, Miss Pringle? Do they make these things only for ornament, should you think?'

'I think it is time you finished that exercise,' was all the governess replied.

'Oh, I've almost done it,' said Mabel, 'and I want just to ask this question (it comes under "general information," you know)—aren't vegetable colours "dilly-whatever-it-is" colours I mean—harmless? And Dr. Harley said vegetables were so very good for me. I wonder if I might just taste him.'

Here the prince's dream ended: he saw it all at last—how she had petted and praised him only while he was pleasant to look at; and now that was over—he was nothing more to her than something to eat.

Presently he was lifted gently between her slim finger and thumb to her lips, and touched caressingly by something red and moist and warm behind them. It was not unpleasant exactly, so far, but he knew that worse was coming, and longed for her to make haste and get it over.

'Vanilla!' reported Mabel, 'that must be all right, Miss Pringle. Cook flavours corn-flour with it!'

Miss Pringle shrugged her sharp shoulders: 'You must use your own judgment, my dear,' was all she said.

And then—I am sorry to have to tell what happened next, but this is a true story and I must go on—then the prince saw Mabel's grey eyes looking at him from under their long lashes with interest for the last time, he saw two gleaming pearly rows closing upon him, he felt a sharp pang, of grief as well as pain, as they crunched him up into small pieces, and he slowly melted away and there was an end of him.

There is a beautiful moral belonging to this story, but it is of no use to print it here, because it only applies to sugar princes—until Mabel is quite grown up.


## THE RETURN OF AGAMEMNON

It was ten years since Agamemnon, the mighty Argive monarch, had left his kingdom (somewhat suddenly, and after a stormy interview with the Queen, as those said who had the best opportunities of knowing), with the avowed intention of going to assist at the siege of Troy.

He had never written once since, but so many reports of his personal daring and his terrible wounds had reached the palace that Clytemnestra would often observe, with a touch of annoyance, that, if not actually dead by that time, he must be nearly as full of holes as a fishing-net.

So that she was scarcely surprised when they broke the intelligence to her one day that he really had gone at last, having fallen, fighting desperately, against the most fearful odds, upon the Trojan plain; and when, a little later, she formally announced to her faithful subjects her betrothal to Ægisthus, her youngest and favourite courtier, they were not surprised in their turn.

They told one another, with ribald facetiousness, that they had rather expected something of the kind.

They were celebrating their Queen's betrothal day with the wildest enthusiasm, for they were a simple affectionate people, and foresaw an impetus to local trade. It had been but a dull time for Argos during those weary ten years, and the city had become well-nigh deserted, as, one by one, all her bravest and her best had left her, to seek, as they poetically put it, 'a soldier's tomb.'

Several married men, in whom no such patriotic enthusiasm had ever been previously suspected, found out that their country required their services, left their wives and their little ones, and started for the field of battle. There were many pushing Argive tradesmen, too, who abandoned their business and sought—not ostentatiously, but with the self-effacement of true heroism—the seat of war upon which their sovereign had been sitting so long; while the real extent of their devotion was seldom appreciated until long after their departure, when it was generally discovered that, in their eagerness, they had left their affairs in the greatest confusion.

And very soon almost the only young men left were mild, unwarlike youths, who were respectable and wore spectacles, while the rest of the male population was composed of equal parts of prattling infants and doddering octogenarians.

This was a melancholy state of things—but then the absent ones wrote such capital letters home, containing such graphic descriptions of camp life and the fiercer excitements of night attacks and forlorn hopes, that the recipients ought to have been amply consoled.

They were not; they only remarked that it seemed rather odd that the writers should so persistently forget to give their addresses, and that it was a singular circumstance that while each letter purported to come direct from the Grecian lines, every envelope somehow bore a different postmark. And often would the older married women (and their mothers too) wish with infinite pathos that they could only just get the missing ones home and talk to them a little—that was all!

But all anxiety was forgotten in the celebration of the betrothal, for the Argives were determined to do the thing really well. So in the principal streets they had erected triumphal arches, typifying the chief local manufactures, which were (as it is scarcely necessary to inform the scholar) soda-water and cane-bottomed chairs; and from these arches chairs and bottles were constantly dropping, like a gentle dew, upon the happy crowd which passed beneath. All the public fountains spouted a cheap dinner sherry like water—'very like water,' said some disaffected persons; householders were graciously invited to exhibit flags and illuminations at their own expense, and in the market-place a fowl was being roasted whole for the populace.

All was gaiety, therefore, at sunset, when the citizens assembled in groups about the square in front of the palace, prepared to cheer the royal pair with enthusiasm when they deigned to show themselves upon the balcony.

The well-meaning old gentlemen who formed the Chorus (for in those days every house of any position in society maintained a chorus, and even shabby-genteel families kept a semi-chorus in buttons) were twittering in a corner, prepared to come forth by-and-by with the ill-timed allusions, melancholy and depressing forebodings, and unnecessary advice, which were all that was expected of them, and the Mayor and Corporation were fussing about distractedly with a brass band and the inevitable address.

All at once there was a stir in the crowd, and the eyes of everyone were strained towards a tall and swaying scaffold on the royal house-top, where a small black figure, outlined sharply against the saffron sky, could be seen gesticulating wildly?

'Look at the watchman!' they whispered excitedly; 'what can be the matter with him?'

Now before Agamemnon left he had had fires laid upon all the mountain tops in a straight line between Argos and Troy, arranging to light the pile at the Troy end of the chain when it should become necessary to let them know at home that they might expect him back shortly.

The watchman had been put up on a scaffold to look out for the beacon, and had been there for years day and night, without being once allowed to quit his post—even on his birthday. It was expected that Clytemnestra would have let him come down for good when she was informed of Agamemnon's death on such excellent authority, but she would not hear of such a thing. She knew people would think it very foolish and sentimental of her, she said, but to take the watchman down would seem so like giving up all hope! So she kept him up, a proof of her conjugal devotion which touched everyone—except perhaps the watchman himself.

Clytemnestra and Ægisthus, who had happened to come out while all this excitement was at its height, found themselves absolutely ignored. 'Not a single cap off—not one solitary hurray,' cried the Queen with majestic anger. 'What have you been doing to make yourself so unpopular with my loyal Argives?' she demanded suspiciously.

'I don't think it's anything to do with me, really,' protested Ægisthus, feebly. 'They're only looking the other way just now, and—can't you see why?' he added suddenly, 'they've lit the beacon on the top of Arachnæus!'

Clytemnestra looked, and started violently, as on the mountain-top in question a red tongue of flame shot up through the gathering dusk: 'What does it mean?' she whispered, clutching him convulsively by the arm.

'Well,' said Ægisthus, 'it looks to me, do you know, rather as if your late lamented husband has changed his mind about dying, and is on his way to your arms.'

'Then he is not dead!' exclaimed Clytemnestra. 'He is coming home. I shall look upon that face, hear that voice, press that hand once again! How excessively annoying!'

'Confounded nuisance!' he agreed heartily, but his irritation sounded slightly overdone, somehow. 'Well, it's all over with the betrothal after this; don't you think it would be as well to get all the arches, and fireworks, and things out of the way? We shan't want them now, you know.'

'Why not?' said the Queen; 'they will all do for him; he won't know. Ye gods!' she cried, stretching out her arms with a tragic groan. 'Must I, too, do for him?'

'Any way,' said Ægisthus, with an attempted ease, 'you won't want me any longer, and so, if you will kindly excuse me, I—I think I'll retire to some quiet spot whither I can drag myself with my broken heart and bleed to death, like a wounded deer, don't you know!'

'You can do all that just as well here,' she replied. 'I wish you to stay. Who knows what may happen?'—she added, with a sinister smile, 'We may be happy yet!'

Clytemnestra's sinister smiles always made Ægisthus feel exactly as if something was disagreeing with him—so he stayed.

By this time the populace had also realised the turn affairs had taken, but they very sensibly determined that it was their plain duty to persevere with the merriment. They were, as has been mentioned before, a simple and affectionate people, and fond of their king; so, as his return would be even more beneficial to trade than the betrothal, they rejoiced on, and there was nothing in the least strained or hollow in their revelry.

And presently there was a fresh stir in the crowd, and then a rumbling of wheels as the covered chariot from the station rolled, amidst faint cheering, up to the palace gates, and was saluted by the one aged sentinel who stood on guard.

'It is Agamemnon,' gasped the Queen; 'he has come already—he must not find me unprepared. I will go within.'

She had just time to retire hastily, followed by Ægisthus, before a short stout man in faded regimentals and a cocked hat with a moulting plume descended from the vehicle.

The Chorus, finding it left to them to do the honours, advanced in a row, singing the ode of welcome, which they had had in rehearsal ever since the first year of the war.

'O King,' they chanted in their cracked old trebles, 'offspring of Atreus, and sacker of Troy!'

'Will you kindly count the boxes?' interrupted the monarch, who hated sentiment; 'there should be four—a tin cocked-hat box, two camel-hair trunks, and a carpet bag.'

But a Greek chorus was not easily suppressed, and they broke out again all together, 'Nay, but with bursting hearts would we bid thee thrice hail!'

'Once is ample, thank you,' said the King, with regal politeness; 'and I should be really distressed if any of you were to burst on my account. Has anybody such a thing as half a drachma about him?'

He heard no more of the ode, and the Mayor thought it advisable to roll up his address and take his Corporation home.

Agamemnon had succeeded in borrowing the drachma, and had just turned his back to pay the driver as Clytemnestra glided down the broad steps to the court-yard, and, striking an attitude, addressed nobody in particular in tones of rapturous joy.

'O happy day!' she cried very loudly, 'on which my hero husband returns to me after a long absence, quite unexpectedly. Henceforth shall his helmet rust upon the hat-stand, and his spear repose innocuous amongst the umbrellas, and his breastplate shall he replace by a chest-protector; for a shield he shall have a sunshade, and instead of his sword he shall carry a spud. But now let me, as an exceptionally faithful wife, greet him before ye all with—Agamemnon, will you have the goodness to tell me who that young person is in the chariot?' was her abrupt and somewhat lame conclusion.

'Oh, there you are, eh?' said Agamemnon, turning round and presenting a forefinger. 'How de do, my love; how de do?' ('I shan't give you another obol!' he said to the driver, who seemed still unsatisfied.) 'So, you're quite well, eh?' he resumed to his wife; 'plenty to say for yourself as usual. Gad, I feel as if I hadn't been away a week—till I look at you.... Well, we can't expect to be always young, can we? So you want to know my little friend here? Allow me to present her to you. One moment.'

And bustling up to the chariot, he assisted from it a maiden with a pale face, great, wild, roving eyes, and hair of tawny gold, and led her back to his wife.

'The Princess Cassandra of Troy—my wife, Queen Clytemnestra. They tell me this young lady can prophesy very prettily, my dear,' he remarked.

Clytemnestra bowed coldly, and said she was sure it would be vastly amusing. Did the Princess intend giving any public entertainments?

'She is our visitor,' Agamemnon put in warningly; while Cassandra smiled satirically, and said nothing at all.

Clytemnestra hoped she might be able to induce her to stay longer, a week was such a very short time.

'She has kindly consented to stay on a little longer, my love,' said Agamemnon—'all her life,' in fact.'

The Queen was charmed to hear it; it was so very nice and kind of her, particularly as strangers were apt to find the neighbourhood an unhealthy one.

And as Ægisthus joined them just then, she presented him to the King, with the remark that he had been the most faithful and devoted of courtiers during the whole period of the King's absence; to which Agamemnon replied, with the slightest of scowls, that he was delighted to make the acquaintance of Mr. Ægisthus; and after that no one seemed to know exactly what to say for a minute or two.

At last Ægisthus hazarded a supposition that the royal warrior had found it warm over at Troy.

'It varied, sir,' said the monarch, uncomfortably; 'the climate varied. I used to get very warm fighting sometimes.'

Ægisthus agreed that a battle must be hot work, and Clytemnestra suddenly exclaimed that her husband was wearing the very same dear shabby old uniform he had on when he went away.

'The very same,' said Agamemnon, smiling. 'I wore it all through the campaign. Your true warrior is no dandy!'

'We were given to understand you were wounded,' remarked Ægisthus.

'Oh,' said the King, 'yes; I was considerably wounded—all over the chest and arms. But what cared I?'

'Exactly,' said Ægisthus; 'and, curiously enough, the weapons don't seem to have pierced your coat at all. I observe there are no patches.'

'No,' the King replied; 'so you noticed that, eh? Well, the reason of that is that those fellows out there have a peculiar sort of way of cutting and slashing, so as to—'

And he explained this by some elaborate illustrations with his sheathed sword, until Ægisthus said that he thought he understood how it was done.

But Clytemnestra suddenly, with a kitten-like girlishness that sat but ill upon her, pounced playfully upon the weapon. 'I want to see it drawn,' she cried; 'I want to look upon the keen flashing blade which has penetrated the inmost recesses of so many of our country's foes. Oh, it won't come out,' she added, as she attempted to pull it out of the scabbard; 'do make it come out!'

The King tried, but the blade stuck half way, and what was visible of it seemed thickly coated with rust; but Agamemnon said it was gore, and his orderly must have forgotten to clean his accoutrements after the fall of Troy. He added that it was the effect of the sea air.

'Troy really has fallen then?' asked Ægisthus. 'I suppose you stayed to see the thing out?'

'I did, sir,' answered the monarch proudly; 'I sacked the most fashionable quarters myself. I expect my booty will be forwarded—shortly. Didn't you know Troy was taken?' he asked suspiciously. 'Couldn't you see the beacon I lighted just before I started?'

The courtier murmured that it was wonderful to find so long and tedious a journey accomplished in such capital time.

'What do you mean by that? How do you know how long it took?' demanded Agamemnon.

'Don't you see?' said Clytemnestra. 'Why, you say you had the fire lighted at Ida when you started; then, of course, they would see it directly over at Lemnos, and light theirs; and then at Athos, and then—'

'You are not a time-table, my love,' interrupted the monarch, coldly. 'I won't trouble you for all these details. Come to the point.'

'The point is,' she explained sweetly, 'that we have only just seen the beacon flame arrive here at Arachnæus, after leaping from height to height across lake and plain; so that you, my dearest, must have made the distance with almost equal celerity!'

'I came with the beacon,' said Agamemnon, coughing; 'perhaps that disposes of the difficulty?'

'Perhaps,' said the Queen; 'I mean quite. And now,' she continued, after a rapid exchange of glances with Ægisthus, 'you will come indoors, and have a nice cup of coffee and a warm bath before you do anything else, won't you?'

He almost thought he would, he said; fighting for ten long years without intermission was a dusty, tiring occupation, and he was accordingly about to enter, when his eye fell on the awnings and flags and the red stair carpet, which had been prepared for the betrothal festivities, and he frowned.

'Now, my dear, this sort of thing is all very well, no doubt; but I don't care about it. I'm a plain, honest ruler of men, and I hate flummery and flattery—particularly when it all comes out of my pocket! Why, you've laid down the drugget from the Throne-Room over all this gravel. Take it up directly; I decline to walk over it. Do you hear? This wasteful extravagance is positively sinful. Take it up!'

Clytemnestra assured him earnestly that they had had no intention of annoying him with it—which was literally true; and suggested meekly that for the King to stay out in the court-yard until all the decorations were removed might be a tedious and even a ridiculous proceeding. 'If,' she added, 'he was merely unwilling to spoil the drugget, he might easily remove his boots, which were extremely muddy—for a monarch's.'

'Well, well, my dear, be it so,' said the King; 'I did not intend to chide you. It is only that I have grown so accustomed to the frugal, hardy life of a camp, that I have imbibed a soldier's contempt for luxury.'

And, removing his boots, he followed the Queen into the Palace, as she led the way with a baleful expression upon her dark and inscrutable face.

As the pair passed up the steps and between the lofty pillars, the hounds howled from the royal kennels at the back of the Palace, and—a stranger portent still—a meteor shot suddenly through the growing gloom and burst in a rain of coloured stars above the house-top, while, shortly after, a staff fell from above upon the head of one of the Chorus—and was shivered to fragments!

Ægisthus had strolled away under the colonnade, and Cassandra was left alone with the Chorus. She stood apart, mystic, moody, and impenetrable, letting down her flowing back hair.

'You prophesy, do you not?' said the kind old men at length, wishing to make her feel at home; 'might we beg you to favour us with a prediction—just a little one?'

Cassandra made excuses at first, as was proper; she had a cold, and was feeling the effects of the journey. She was really not inspired just then, she protested, and besides, she had not touched a tripod for ages.

But, upon being pressed, she gave way at last, after declaring with a little giggle that she was perfectly certain nobody would believe a single word she said.

'I see before me,' she began, in a weird, sepulchral tone which she found it impossible to keep up for many sentences, 'a proud and stately pile—but enter not. See ye yon ghoul among the chimney-pots, yon amphisboena in the back garden? And the scent of gore pervades it!'

'It is no happy home that is thus described!' the Chorus threw in profesionally.

'But the Finger of Fate is slowly unwound, and the Hand of Destiny steps in to pace the marble halls with heavy tramp. And know, old men, that the Inevitable is not wholly unconnected with the Probable!'

At this even their politeness could not restrain a gesture of incredulity, but she heeded it not, and continued:

'Who is this that I see next—this regal warrior bounding over the blazing battlements in brazen panoply?'

('That must be Agamemnon,' cried the Chorus; 'the despatches mentioned him bounding like that. Wonderful!')

'I see him,' she resumed, 'pale and prostrate—a prey to the pangs within him, scanning the billows from his storm-tossed ship. Now he has reached his native city. Hark! how they greet him! And, behold, a stately matron meets him with a honeyed smile, inviting him to enter. He yields. And then—'

Here Cassandra stopped, with the remark that that was all—as there were limits even to the marvellous faculty of second-sight.

The Chorus were not unimpressed, for they had never seen a prediction and its literal fulfilment in quite such close conjunction before, and their own attempts always came wrong; but although they were agreed that the prophecy was charming as far as it went, they began to feel slightly afraid of the prophetess, and were secretly relieved when Ægisthus happened to come up shortly afterwards with an offer to show her such places of interest as Argos boasted.

But they were great authorities upon all points of etiquette and morality, and they all remarked (when she had gone) that she displayed an unbecoming readiness in accepting the escort of a courtier who had not been formally introduced to her. 'That may be the custom in Troy,' they said, wagging their beards, 'but if she means to behave like that here—well!'

And now the last gleam of the sunset had faded, and the stars straggled out in the pale green sky, whilst the Chorus walked up and down to keep warm, for the evening was growing chilly.

Suddenly a loud cry broke the silence—a scream as of a strong man in mortal agony! It struck all of them that the voice was uncommonly like Agamemnon's, but none liked to say so, and they only observed with a forced composure that really the cats were becoming quite a nuisance.

The cry came again, louder this time, and more distinct; it seemed to come from the direction of the royal bath-room. 'Hi, here, somebody—help! They've turned on the hot water, and I can't turn it off again!'

After this there could be no possible doubt that there was something the matter far more serious than cats. Agamemnon, the king of men, was apparently in difficulties, and it was only too probable that this was Clytemnestra's fell work.

They all ran about and fell over one another in the general flurry and confusion, and then as they recovered their presence of mind they began to consult upon the best course to pursue under the circumstances. Some were of opinion that it would not be a quite unpardonable breach of court etiquette if they were to rush into the bath-room and pull the royal sufferer out; others, more cautious, asked for precedents in a case of such delicacy, and they almost quarrelled, until the wisest of them all reminded his fellows that, at all events, it was too late to interfere then, as the monarch must certainly be hard-boiled by that time—which relieved them from all responsibility in the happiest manner.

At this point the Queen appeared at the head of the marble steps, down which she glided cautiously and came towards them, evidently in a condition of suppressed excitement.

'What a beautiful evening!' said the Chorus in unison, for they considered it better taste not to appear to have noticed anything at all unusual.

'Agamemnon is with his ancestors,' she replied in a fierce whisper; 'I sewed up the sleeves of his bathing-gown and I drugged his coffee, and then from afar I turned on the hot water. And he is boiled, and it serves him right, and I'm glad of it—so now! But tell me, ye aged ones,' she added with one of her quick transitions, 'have I done well?'

Now the Chorus were distinctly disgusted at her want of tact and reserve, and would have greatly preferred not to be admitted into confidences of so purely domestic a description, but they were not the men to flinch from their duty.

'In our opinion, O Queen,' they replied coldly, 'the deed was a hasty one, and accomplished without sufficient consideration.'

'Ha!' she exclaimed angrily, 'so ye would rate me like a girl! Am I not your sovereign mistress? Guard, seize these insolents!'

And the superannuated old sentinel left his box and tottered up to seize as many of them as he could lay hold of at once, telling the remainder to consider themselves under arrest, which they did directly.

'Summon the populace,' Clytemnestra next commanded, and the Argives left the fireworks obediently and assembled before the steps.

'Citizens! Argives!' she cried in a loud clear voice, 'I am sure you will all be very sorry and disappointed to hear that your beloved sovereign, so lately restored to us' (here she broke down with the naturalness of a great artist)—'that our beloved sovereign is—by a most deplorable and unaccountable lack of precaution—'

'Alive!' interrupted a voice from behind the Queen, and someone pushed aside the hangings before the door of the Palace, and began to descend the steps. It was Agamemnon himself.

Clytemnestra shrieked as she turned slowly, and confronted him in silence for some moments; the situation was intensely dramatic, and the Argives, a simple and affectionate people, fully appreciated this, and never once regretted the fireworks they had abandoned.

The Queen was the first to speak: 'So,' she said, pale and panting, 'you—you've—had your bath?'

'Well—no,' said Agamemnon mildly; 'I happened to observe that someone had thoughtfully sewn up the armholes of my dressing-gown, and that the coffee had a particularly nasty smell in it, and so, somehow, I thought I would rather wait. And then the boiling water came rushing in, and I saw there had been a little mistake somewhere. So it occurred to me that I too would dissemble and see what came of it, and I shouted for help. I think I see it all now.'

And then he took a higher moral tone; his manner was no longer cynical; he was not angry even—only deeply wounded, and there was something fine and striking in the stern sadness of his brow.

'So this,' he said, 'was to have been my fate? I was to return, a war-worn warrior, to the hearth and home from which I had been absent so long—so long—to be ruthlessly parboiled the very moment after my arrival, by the partner of my throne! Was this kind—was this wifely, Clytemnestra?'

'That comes so well from you, does it not?' she retorted.

'Why—why—what do you mean?' he stammered.

'You know very well what I mean,' she said. 'Bah! why play the hypocrite with me?'

'Is it possible,' he cried, 'that you can suspect me of not having been near Troy all this time—tell me, Clytemnestra—is this monstrous thing possible?'

'Quite,' she replied; 'I know you haven't!'

'What—when I tell you that there is a poet, a fellow called Homer or something, who has got a sort of reputation already by putting the campaign into verses, rather long, but quite readable (you must order them); well, there's a lot about me in them.'

'Did Homer see you there?'

'Now that's a most ridiculous question,' he protested, with a feeling that she was coming round, and that he should convince her directly; 'the poet's blind, Clytemnestra, quite blind. But I will not argue— you must be content with a warrior's assurance.'

She laughed. 'I'm afraid,' she said, 'that even a warrior's assurance will find it difficult to account satisfactorily for this—and this—and these!' And as she spoke, she handed him a variety of articles: a folding hat, a guide to Corinth, a conversation manual, several unused tourist tickets, one or two theatre programmes, a green veil, some supper bills, a correct card for the Olympian races, with the names of probable starters, and three little jointed wooden dolls.

Agamemnon took them all helplessly; all his virtuous indignation had evaporated, and he looked very red and foolish as he said with a kind of nervous laugh, 'You've been looking in my pockets!'

'I have,' she said, 'and now what have you to say for yourself? I don't believe there is any such place as Troy.'

'There is indeed,' he pleaded; 'I can show it to you on the map!'

'Well,' she said, 'if there is, you never went near it!'

'Send those people away,' he said, 'and I will tell you all!'

And when they had gone, he confessed everything, explaining that he really had meant to go to Troy at first, and how, as he got nearer, he found himself less and less inclined for fighting—until at last he determined to travel about and see life instead, and, as he expressed it, 'pick up a little character.'

'Well,' said Clytemnestra, 'I will have no little characters in my palace, Agamemnon.'

But he protested that she had not understood him. 'And if I have erred, my love,' he suggested humbly, 'excuse me, but I cannot help thinking that the means devised for my correction were unnecessarily severe!'

'They were nothing of the sort,' she said; 'you deserved it all—and worse!'

Upon this Agamemnon made haste to assure her that she had shown a very proper spirit, and he respected her the more for it. 'And now,' he put it to her, 'why not let bygones be bygones?' But Clytemnestra's reply was that she would be quite willing to permit this when they were bygones, which, at present, she added, they were very far from being.

The King was in despair, until beneficent nature came to his assistance; a faint chirrup was heard from a neighbouring bush, a circumstance which he turned to admirable account.

'You hear it?' he asked tenderly, 'the dulcet strain? Know ye the note? Ah, Clytemnestra, 'tis the owl— the blithe and tuneful owl! Owls sang on our bridal night—can you hear their melody now and be unmoved? No, I did but wrong ye ... a tear trembles on that eyelash, a smile flickers upon that lip! I am pardoned. Clytemnestra—wife, embrace me ... we both have much to forgive!'

This speech (which was not unlike some he had heard in thrilling dramas at the 'Hæmabronteion,' Corinth, where the prophetess Cassandra had been greatly admired in her impersonations of persecuted and distracted heroines) touched Clytemnestra's heart, in which, hard as it was, there was a strain of sentiment—and she fell sobbing into her husband's arms.

And so all was forgotten and forgiven in the most satisfactory manner, the Chorus (who had been considering themselves arrested until the intellectual strain had proved almost too much for them) were released, while it was found on inquiry that both Ægisthus and Cassandra were missing, and no trace of either of them was ever found again; but it was generally understood that, with a delicate unselfishness, they had been unwilling to remain where their presence would lead to inevitable complications.

And from that night—until the fatal day, some six short weeks afterwards, when each, by an unfortunate oversight, partook of a mixture which had been carefully prepared for the other—there was not a happier royal couple in all Argos than Clytemnestra and Agamemnon.


## THE WRAITH OF BARNJUM

I frankly admit, whatever may be the consequences of doing so, that I was not fond of Barnjum; in fact, I detested him. Everything that fellow said and did jarred upon me to an absolutely indescribable extent, although I did not discover for some time that he regarded me with a strange and unreasonable aversion.

We were so essentially unlike in almost every particular—I, with my innate refinement and high culture, my over-fastidious exclusiveness in the choice of associates; and he, a big, red, coarse brute, with neither sweetness nor light, who knew himself a Philistine, and seemed to like it—we were so unlike, that I often asked him, with a genuine desire for information, what had I in common with him?

And yet it will scarcely be believed, perhaps, that with such good reasons for keeping apart, we were continually seeking one another's company with a zest that knew no satiety. The only explanation I can offer for such a phenomenon is, that our mutual antipathy had become so much a part of ourselves, that we could not let it perish for lack of nourishment.

Perhaps we were not conscious of this at the time, and when we agreed to go on a walking tour together in North Wales, I think it was chiefly because we knew that we could devise no surer means of annoying one another; but, however that may be, in an ill-starred day for my own peace of mind, we started upon a journey from which but one of us was fated to return.

I pass by the painful experiences of the first few days of that unhappy tour. I will say nothing of Barnjum's grovelling animalism, of his consummate selfishness, his more than bucolic indifference to the charms of Nature, nor even of the mean and sordid way in which he contrived to let me in for railway tickets and hotel bills.

I wish to tell my melancholy story with perfect impartiality, and I am sure that I am not reduced to exciting any prejudice to secure the sympathies of all readers.

I shall pass, then, to the memorable day when my disgust, so long pent up, so imperfectly concealed, culminated in one grand outburst of a not ignoble indignation, to the hour when I summoned up moral courage to sever the bonds which linked us so unequally.

I remember it so well, that brilliant morning in June when we left the Temperance Hotel, Doldwyddlm, and scaled in sulky silence the craggy heights of Cader Idris, which, I presume, still overhang that picturesque village, while, as we ascended, an ever-changing and ever-improving panorama unrolled itself before my delighted eyes.

The air up there was keen and bracing, and I recollect that I could not repress an æsthetic shudder at the crude and primitive tone which Barnjum's nose had assumed under atmospheric influences. I mentioned this (for we still maintained the outward forms of friendship), when he retorted, with the brutal personality which formed so strong an ingredient of his character, that if I could only see myself in that suit of mine, and that hat (referring to the dress I was then wearing), I should feel the propriety of letting his nose alone. To which I replied, with a sarcasm that I feel now was a little too crushing, that I had every intention of doing so, as it was quite painful enough to merely contemplate such a spectacle; and he, evidently meaning to be offensive, remarked, that no one could help his nose getting red, but that any man in my position could at least dress like a gentleman I took no notice of this insult; a Bunting (I don't think I mentioned before that my name is Philibert Bunting)—a Bunting can afford to pass such insinuations by; indeed, I find it actually cheaper to do so, and I flattered myself that my dress was distinguished by a sort of studied looseness, that would appeal at once to a cultivated and artistic eye, though of course Barnjum's hard and shallow organs could not be expected to appreciate it.

I overlooked it, then, and presently we found ourselves skirting the edge of a huge chasm, whose steep sides sloped sheer down into the slate-blue waters of the lake below.

How can I hope to give an idea of the magnificent view which met our eyes as we stood there—a view of which, as far as I am aware, no description has ever yet been attempted?

To our right towered the Peaks of Dolgelly, with their saw-like outline cutting the blue sky with a faint grating sound, while the shreds of white cloud lay below in drifts. At our feet were the sun-lit waters of the lake, upon which danced a fleet of brown-sailed herring-boats; beyond was the plain of Capel Curig, and there, over on the left, sparkled the falls of Y-Dydd.

As I took all this in I felt a longing to say something worthy of the occasion. Being possessed of a considerable fund of carefully-dried and selected humour, I frequently amuse myself by a species of intellectual exercise, which consists in so framing a remark that a word or more therein may bear two entirely opposite constructions; and some of the quaint names of the vicinity seemed to me just then admirably adapted for this purpose.

I was about to gauge my dull-witted companion's capacity by some such test, when he forestalled me.

'You ought to live up here, Bunting,' said he; 'you were made for this identical old mountain.'

I was not displeased, for, Londoner as I am, I have the nerve and steadiness of a practised mountaineer.

'Perhaps I was,' I said good-humouredly; 'but how did you find it out?'

'I'll tell you,' he replied, with one of his odious grins. 'This is Cader Idris, ain't it? well, and you're a cad awry dressed, ain't you? Cader Idrissed, see?' (he was dastard enough to explain) 'That's how I get at it!'

He must have been laboriously leading up to that for the last ten minutes!

I solemnly declare that it was not the personal outrage that roused me; I simply felt that a paltry verbal quibble of that description, emitted amidst such scenery and at that altitude, required a protest in the name of indignant Nature, and I protested accordingly, although with an impetuosity which I afterwards regretted, and of which I cannot even now entirely approve.

He happened to be standing on the brink of an abyss, and had just turned his back upon me, as, with a vigorous thrust of my right foot, I launched him into the blue æther, with the chuckle at his unhallowed jest still hovering upon his lips.

I am aware that by such an act I took a liberty which, under ordinary circumstances, even the licence of a life-long friendship would scarcely have justified; but I thought it only due to myself to let him see plainly that I desired our acquaintanceship to cease from that instant, and Barnjum was the kind of man upon whom a more delicate hint would have been distinctly thrown away.

I watched his progress with some interest as he rebounded from point to point during his descent. I waited—punctiliously, perhaps, until the echoes he had aroused had died away on the breeze, and then, slowly and thoughtfully, I retraced my steps, and left a spot which was already becoming associated for me with memories the reverse of pleasurable.

I took the next up-train, and before I reached town had succeeded in dismissing the incident from my mind, or if I thought of it at all, it was only to indulge relief at the reflection that I had shaken off Barnjum for ever.

But when I had paid my cab, and was taking out my latch-key, a curious thing happened—the driver called me back.

'Beg pardon, sir,' he said hoarsely, 'but I think you've bin and left something white in my cab!'

I turned and looked in: there, grinning at me from the interior of the hansom, over the folding-doors, was the wraith of Barnjum!

I had presence of mind enough to thank the man for his honesty, and go upstairs to my rooms with as little noise as possible. Barnjum's ghost, as I expected, followed me in, and sat down coolly before the fire, in my arm-chair, thus giving me an opportunity of subjecting the apparition to a thorough examination.

It was quite the conventional ghost, filmy, transparent, and, though wanting firmness in outline, a really passable likeness of Barnjum. Before I retired to rest I had thrown both my boots and the contents of my bookcase completely through the thing, without appearing to cause it more than a temporary inconvenience—which convinced me that it was indeed a being from another world.

Its choice of garments struck me even then as decidedly unusual. I am not narrow; I cheerfully allow that, assuming the necessity for apparitions at all, it is well that they should be clothed in robes of some kind; but Barnjum's ghost delighted in a combination of costume which set the fitness of things at defiance.

It wore that evening, for instance, to the best of my recollection, striped pantaloons, a surplice, and an immense cocked hat; but on subsequent occasions its changes of costume were so rapid and eccentric, that I ceased to pay much attention to them, and could only explain them on the supposition that somewhere in space there exists a supernatural store in the nature of a theatrical wardrobe, and that Barnjum's ghost had the run of it.

I had not been in very long before my landlady came up to see if I wanted anything, and of course as soon as she came in, she saw the wraith. At first she objected to it very strongly, declaring that she would not have such nasty things in her house, and if I wanted to keep ghosts, I had better go somewhere else; but I pacified her at last by representing that it would give her no extra trouble, and that I was only taking care of it for a friend.

When she had gone, however, I sat up till late, thinking calmly over my position, and the complications which might be expected to ensue from it.

It would be very easy to harrow the reader's feelings and work upon his sympathies here by a telling description of my terror and my guilty confusion at the unforeseen consequences of what I had done. But I think, in relating an experience of this kind, the straightforward way is always the best, and I do not care to heighten the effect by attributing to myself a variety of sensations which I do not remember to have actually felt at the time.

My first impression had not unnaturally been that the spectre was merely the product of overwrought nerves or indigestion, but it seemed improbable that a cabman should be plagued by a morbid activity of imagination, and that a landlady's digestion could be delicate sufficiently to evolve a thing so far removed from the merely commonplace; and, reluctantly enough, I was forced to the conclusion that it was a real ghost, and would probably continue to haunt me to the end of my days.

Of course I was disgusted by this exhibition of petty revenge and low malice on the part of Barnjum, which might be tolerated perhaps in a Christmas annual, with a full-page illustration, but which, in real life and the height of summer, was a glaring anachronism.

Still, it was of no use to repine then; I resolved to look at the thing in a common-sense light—I told myself that I had made my ghost, and would have to live with it. And after all, I had much to be thankful for: Barnjum in the spirit was a decided improvement upon Barnjum in the flesh; and as the spirit did not appear to be gifted with speech, it was unlikely to tell tales.

Luckily for me, too, Barnjum was absolutely unknown about town: his only relative was an aunt resident at Camberwell, and so there was no danger of any suspicion being excited by chance recognition in the circles to which I belonged.

It would have been folly to shut one's eyes to the fact that it might require considerable nerve to re-enter society closely attended by an obscure and fancifully-attired apparition.

Society would sneer considerably at first and make remarks, but I was full of tact and knowledge of the world, and I knew, too, that men have overcome far more formidable obstacles to social success than any against which I should be called upon to contend.

And so, instead of weakly giving way to unreasonable panic, I took the more manly course of determining to live it down, with what success I shall have presently to show.

When I went out after breakfast the next morning, Barnjum's ghost insisted upon coming too, and followed me, to my intense annoyance, all down St. James's Street; in fact, for many weeks it was almost constantly by my side, and rendered me the innocent victim of mingled curiosity and aversion.

I thought it best to affect to be unaware of the presence of anything of a ghostly nature, and when taxed with it, ascribed it to the diseased fancy of my interlocutor; but, by-and-by, as the whole town began to ring with the story, I found it impossible to pretend ignorance any longer.

So I gave out that it was an artfully-contrived piece of spectral mechanism, of which I was the inventor, and for which I contemplated taking out a patent; and this would have earned for me a high reputation in the scientific world if Messrs. Maskelyne and Cooke had not grown envious of my fame, declaring that they had long since anticipated the secret of my machine, and could manufacture one in every way superior to it, which they presently did.

Then I was obliged to confide (in the strictest secrecy) to two members of the Peerage (both persons of irreproachable breeding, with whom I was at that time exceedingly intimate) that it was indeed a bonâ fide apparition, and that I rather liked such things about me. I cannot explain how it happened, but in a very short time the story had gone the round of the clubs and drawing-rooms, and I found myself launched as a lion of the largest size—if it is strictly correct to speak of launching a lion.

I received invitations everywhere, on the tacit understanding that I was to bring my ghost, and the wraith of Barnjum, as some who read this may remember, was to be seen at all the best houses in town for the remainder of the season; while in the following autumn, I was asked down for the shooting by several wealthy parvenus, with a secret hope, unless I am greatly mistaken, that the ghost might conceive the idea of remaining with them permanently, thereby imparting to their brand-new palaces the necessary flavour of legend and mystery; but of course it never did.

To tell the truth, whatever novelty there was about it soon wore off—too soon, in fact, for, fickle as society is, I have no hesitation in asserting that we ought to have lasted it at least a second season, if only Barnjum's ghost had not persisted in making itself so ridiculously cheap that, in little more than a fortnight, society was as sick of it as I was myself.

And then the inconveniences which attached to my situation began to assert themselves more and more emphatically.

I began to stay at home sometimes in the evening, when I observed that the phantom had an unpleasant trick of illuminating itself at the approach of darkness with a bilious green light, which, as it was not nearly strong enough to enable me to dispense with a reading lamp, merely served to depress me.

And then it began to absent itself occasionally for days together, and though at first I was rather glad not to see so much of it, I grew uneasy at last. I was always fancying that the Psychical Society, who are credited with understanding the proper treatment of spectres in health and disease, from the tomb upwards, might have got hold of it and be teaching it to talk and compromise me. I heard afterwards that one of their most prominent members did happen to come across it, but, with a scepticism which I cannot but think was somewhat wanting in discernment, rejected it as a palpable imposition.

I had to leave the rooms where I had been so comfortable, for my landlady complained that the street was blocked up by a mob of the lowest description from seven till twelve every evening, and she really could not put up with it any longer.

On inquiry I found that this was owing to Barnjum's ghost getting out upon the roof almost every night after dark, and playing the fool among the chimney-pots, causing me, as its apparent owner, to be indicted five times for committing a common nuisance by obstructing the thoroughfare, and once for collecting an unlawful assembly: I spent all my spare cash in fines.

I believe there were portraits of us both in the 'Illustrated Police News,' but the distinction implied in this was more than outweighed by the fact that Barnjum's wraith was slowly but surely undermining both my fortune and my reputation.

It followed me one day to one of the underground railway stations, and would get into a compartment with me, which led to a lawsuit that made a nine days' sensation in the legal world. I need only mention the celebrated case of 'The Metropolitan District Railway v. Bunting,' in which the important principle was once for all laid down that a railway company by the terms of its contract is entitled to refuse to carry ghosts, spectres, or any other supernatural baggage, and can moreover exact a heavy penalty from passengers who infringe its bye-laws in this respect.

This was, of course, a decision against me, and carried heavy costs, which my private fortune was just sufficient to meet.

But Barnjum's ghost was bent upon alienating me from society also, for at one of the best dances of the season, at a house where I had with infinite pains just succeeded in establishing a precarious footing, that miserable phantom disgraced me for ever by executing a shadowy but decidedly objectionable species of cancan between the dances!

Feeling indirectly responsible for its behaviour, I apologised profusely to my hostess, but the affair found its way into the society journals, and she never either forgave or recognised me again.

Shortly after that, the committee of my club (one of the most exclusive in London) invited me to resign, intimating that, by introducing an acquaintance of questionable antecedents and disreputable exterior into the smoking-room, I had abused the privileges of membership.

I had been afraid of this when I saw it following me into the building, arrayed in Highland costume and a tall hat; but I was quite unable to drive it away.

Up to that time I had been at the bar, where I was doing pretty well, but now no respectable firm of solicitors would employ a man who had such an unprofessional thing as a phantom about his chambers. I threw up my practice, and had no sooner changed my last sovereign than I was summoned for keeping a ghost without a licence!

Some men, no doubt, would have given up there and then in despair—but I am made of sterner stuff, and, besides, an idea had already occurred to me of turning the table upon my shadowy persecutor.

Barnjum's ghost had ruined me: why should I not endeavour to turn an honest penny out of Barnjum's ghost? It was genuine—as I well knew; it was, in some respects, original; it was eminently calculated to delight the young and instruct the old; there was even a moral or two to be got out of it, and though it had long failed to attract in town, I saw no reason why it should not make a great hit in the provinces.

I borrowed the necessary funds and had soon made all preliminary arrangements for running the wraith of Barnjum on a short tour in the provinces, deciding to open at Tenby, in South Wales.

I took every precaution, travelling by night and keeping within doors all day, lest the shade (which was deplorably destitute of the commonest professional pride) should get about and exhibit itself beforehand for nothing; and so successful was I, that when it first burst upon a Welsh audience, from the platform of the Assembly Rooms, Tenby, no ghost could have wished for a more enthusiastic reception, and—for the first and last time—I felt positively proud of it!

But the applause gradually subsided, and was succeeded by an awkward pause. It had not struck me till that moment that it would be necessary to do or say anything in particular during the exhibition, beyond showing the spectators round the phantom, and making the customary assurance that there was no deception and no concealed machinery, which I could do with a clear conscience. But a terrible conviction struck me as I stood there bowing repeatedly, that the audience had come prepared for a comic duologue, with incidental music and dances.

This was quite out of the question, even supposing that Barnjum's ghost would have helped me to entertain them, which, perhaps, I could scarcely expect. As it was, it did nothing at all, except grimace at the audience and make an idiotic fool of itself and me—an exhibition of which they soon wearied. I am perfectly certain that an ordinary magic lantern would have made a far deeper impression upon them.

Whether the wraith managed in some covert way, when my attention was diverted, to insult the national prejudices of that sensitive and hot-blooded nation, I cannot say. All I know is, that after sitting still for some time they suddenly rose as one man; chairs were hurled at me through the ghost, and the stage was completely wrecked before the audience could be induced to go away.

It was all over. I was hopelessly ruined now! My weak fancy that even a spectre would have some remnants of common decency and good-feeling hanging about it, had put the finishing touch to my misfortunes!

I paid for the smashed platform and windows with the money that had been taken at the doors, and then I travelled back to London, third class, that night, with the feeling that everything was against me.

It was Christmas, and I was sitting gloomily in my shabby Bloomsbury lodgings, watching with a miserable, apathetic interest Barnjum's wraith as, clad in a Roman toga, topboots, and a turban, it flitted about the horsehair furniture.

I was wondering if they would admit me into any workhouse while the spectre continued my attendant; I was utterly and completely wretched, and now, for the first time, I really repented my conduct in having parted with Barnjum so abruptly by the bleak cliff side, that bright June morning.

I had heard no more of him—I knew he must have reached the bottom after his fall, because I heard the splash he made—but no tidings had come of the discovery of his body; the lake kept its dark secret well.

If I could only hope that this insidious shade, now that it had hounded me down to poverty, would consider this as a sufficient expiation of my error and go away and leave me in peace! But I felt, only too keenly, that it was one of those one-idea'd apparitions, which never know when they have had enough of a good thing—it would be sure to stay and see the very last of me!

All at once there came a sharp tap at my door, and another figure strode solemnly in. This, too, wore the semblance of Barnjum, but was cast in a more substantial mould, and possessed the power of speech, as I gathered from its addressing me instantly as a cowardly villain.

I started back, and stood behind an arm-chair, facing those two forms, the shadow and the solid, with a feeling of sick despair. 'Listen to me,' I said, 'both of you: so long as your—your original proprietor was content with a single wraith, I put up with it; I did not enjoy myself—but I endured it. But a brace of apparitions is really carrying the thing too far; it's more than any one man's fair allowance, and I won't stand it. I defy the pair of you. I will find means to escape you. I will leave the world! Other people can be ghosts as well as you—it's not a monopoly! If you don't go directly, I shall blow my brains out!'

There was no firearm of any description in the house, but I was too excited for perfect accuracy.

'Blow your brains out by all means!' said the solid figure; 'I don't know what all this nonsense you're talking is about. I'm not a ghost that I'm aware of; I'm alive (no thanks to you); and, to come back to the point—scoundrel!'

'Barnjum—and alive!' I cried, almost with relief. 'If that is so,' I added, feeling that I had been imposed upon in a very unworthy and ungentlemanly manner, 'will you have the goodness to tell me what right you have to this ridiculous apparition here?'

He did not seem to have noticed it particularly till then. 'Hullo!' he said, looking at it with some curiosity, 'what d'ye call that thing?'

'I call it a beastly nuisance!' I said. 'Ever since—since I last saw you, it's been following me about everywhere in a—in a very annoying manner!'

Will it be believed that the unfeeling brute only chuckled at this? 'I don't know anything about it,' he said, 'but all I can say is that it serves you jolly well right, and I hope it will go on annoying you.'

'This is ungenerous,' I said, determined to appeal to any better feelings he might have; 'we did not part on—on the best of terms perhaps—'

'Considering that you kicked me over a precipice when I wasn't looking,' he retorted brutally, 'we may take that as admitted.'

'But, at all events,' I argued, 'it is ridiculous to cherish an old grudge all this time; you must see the absurdity of it yourself.'

'No, I don't,' he said.

I determined to make a last effort to move him. 'It is Christmas Eve, Barnjum,' I said earnestly, 'Christmas Eve. Think of it. At this hour, thousands of throbbing human hearts are speeding the cheap but genial Christmas card to such of their relations as they consider at all likely to respond with a turkey. The costermonger, imaginative for the nonce, is investing damaged evergreens with a purely fictitious value, and the cheery publican is sending the member of his village goose-club back to his cottage home, rich in the possession of a shot-distended bird and a bottle of poisonous port. Hear my appeal. If I was hasty with you, I have been punished. That detestable thing on the hearthrug there has dogged my path to misery and ruin; you cannot be without some responsibility for its conduct. I ask you now, as a man— nay, as an individual—to call it off. You can do it well enough if you only choose; you know you can.'

But Barnjum wouldn't; he only looked at his own wraith with a grim satisfaction as it capered in an imbecile fashion upon the rug.

'Do,' I implored him; 'I would do it for you, Barnjum. I've had it about me for six months, and I am so sick of it.'

Still he hesitated. Some waits outside were playing one of those pathetic American melodies—I forget now whether it was 'Silver Threads among the Gold,' or 'In the Sweet By-and-By'—but, at all events, they struck some sympathetic chord in Barnjum's rough bosom, for his face began to twitch, and presently he burst unexpectedly into tears.

'You don't deserve it,' he said between his sobs, 'but be it so'; then, turning to the ghost, he added: Here, you, what's your name? avaunt! D'ye hear, hook it!'

It wavered for an instant, and then, to my joy, it suddenly 'gave' all over, and, shrivelling up into a sort of cobweb, was drawn by the draught into the fireplace, and carried up the chimney, and I never saw it again.

Barnjum's escape was very simple; he had fallen upon one of the herring-boats in the lake, and the heap of freshly-caught fish lying on the deck had merely broken his fall instead of his neck. As soon as he had recovered from the effects, he was called away from this country upon urgent business, and found himself unable to return for months.

But to this day the appearance of the wraith is a mystery to me. If Barnjum had been the kind of man to be an 'esoteric Buddhist,' it might be accounted for as an 'astral shape'; but esoteric Buddhism requires an exemplary character and years of abstract meditation—both of which conditions were far beyond Barnjum's attainment.

The shape may have been one of those subtle emanations which we are told some people are constantly shedding, like the coats of an onion, and which certain conditions of the atmosphere, and the extreme activity of Barnjum's mind under sudden excitement, possibly contributed to materialise in this particular instance.

Or, perhaps, it was merely a caprice of one of those vagrant Poltergeists, or supernatural buffoons, which took upon itself, very officiously, the duty of avenging my behaviour to Barnjum.

Upon one point I am clear: the whole of this system of deliberate persecution being undertaken directly on Barnjum's account, he is morally and legally bound to reimburse me for the heavy expense and damage which have resulted therefrom.

Hitherto I have been unable to impress Barnjum with this principle, and so my wrongs are still without redress.

I may be asked why I do not make them the basis of an action at law; but persons of any refinement will understand my reluctance to resort to legal proceedings against one with whom I have at least lived on a footing of friendship. I would fain persuade, and shrink from appealing to force; and, besides, I have not succeeded as yet in persuading any solicitor—even a shady one—to take up my case.


A TOY TRAGEDY

This story is mostly about dolls, and I am afraid that all boys, and a good many girls who have tried hard to forget that they ever had dolls, will not care about hearing it. Still, as I have been very careful to warn them at the very beginning, they must not blame me if they read on and find that it does not interest them.

It was after dark, and the criss-cross shadows of the high wire-fender were starting in and out on the walls and ceiling of Winifred's nursery in the flickering firelight, and Winifred's last new doll Ethelinda was sitting on the top of a chest of drawers, leaning back languidly against the wall.

Ethelinda was a particularly handsome doll; she had soft thick golden hair, arranged in the latest fashion, full blue eyes, with rather more expression in them than dolls' eyes generally have, a rose-leaf complexion, the least little haughty curl on her red lips, and a costume that came direct from Paris.

She ought to have been happy with all these advantages, and yet she was plainly dissatisfied; she looked disgustedly at all around her, at the coloured pictures from the illustrated papers on the walls, the staring red dolls' house, the big Noah's ark on the shelf, and the dingy dappled rocking-horse in the corner—she despised them all.

'I do wish I was back in Regent Street again,' she sighed aloud.

There was another doll sitting quite close to her, but Ethelinda had not made the remark to him, as he did not seem at all the sort of person to be encouraged.

He was certainly odd-looking: his head was a little too big for his body, and his body was very much too big for his legs; he had fuzzy white hair, and a face which was rather like Punch's only with all the fun taken out of it.

When anyone pinched him in the chest hard, he squeaked and shut his eyes, as if it hurt him—and very likely it did. He wore a tawdry jester's dress of red and blue, and once he had even carried a cymbal in each hand and clapped them together every time they made him squeak; but he had always disliked being obliged to make so much noise, for he was of a quiet and retiring nature, and so he had got rid of his unmusical instruments as soon as he could.

Still, even without the cymbals, his appearance was hardly respectable, and Ethelinda was a little annoyed to find him so near her, though he never guessed her feelings, which was fortunate for him, for he had fallen in love with her.

Since he first entered the nursery he had had a good deal of knocking about, but his life there had begun to seem easier to put up with from the moment she formed part of it.

He had never dared to speak to her before, she had never given him the chance; and besides, it was quite enough for him to look at her; but now he thought she meant to be friendly and begin a conversation.

'Are you very dull here then?' he asked rather nervously.

Ethelinda stared at first; no one had introduced him, and she felt very much inclined to take no notice; however, she thought after her long silence that it might amuse her to talk to somebody, even if it was only a shabby common creature like this jester.

So she said, 'Dull! You were never in Regent Street, or you wouldn't ask such a question.'

'I came from the Lowther Arcade,' he said.

'Oh, really?' drawled Ethelinda; 'then, of course, this would be quite a pleasant change for you.'

'I don't know,' he said; 'I liked the Arcade. It was so lively; a little noisy perhaps—too much top spinning, and pop-gunning, and mouth-organ playing all round one—but very cheerful. Yes, I liked the Arcade.'

'Very mixed the society there, isn't it?' she asked; 'aren't you expected to know penny things?'

'Well, there were a good many penny things there,' he owned, 'and very amusing they were. There was a wooden bird there that used to duck his head and wag his tail when they swung a weight underneath—he would have made you laugh so!'

'I hope,' said Ethelinda freezingly, 'I should never so far forget myself as to laugh under any circumstances—and certainly not at a penny thing!'

'I wonder how much he cost?' she thought; 'not very much, I can see from his manner. But perhaps I can get him to tell me. Do you remember,' she asked aloud, 'what was the—ah—the premium they asked for introducing you here—did you happen to catch the amount?

'Do you mean my price?' he said; 'oh, elevenpence three farthings—it was on the ticket.'

'What a vulgar creature!' thought Ethelinda; 'I shall really have to drop him.'

'Dear me,' she said,'that sounds very reasonable, very moderate indeed; but perhaps you were "reduced"?' for she thought he would be more bearable if he had cost a little more once.

'I don't think so,' he said; 'that's the fair selling price.'

'Well, that's very curious,' said she, 'because the young man at Regent Street (a most charming person, by the way) positively wouldn't part with me under thirty-five shillings, and he said so many delightful things about me that I feel quite sorry for him sometimes, when I think how he must be missing me. But then, very likely he's saying the same thing about some other doll now!'

'I suppose he is,' said the jester (he had seen something of toy-selling in his time); 'it's his business, you know.'

'I don't see how you can possibly tell,' said Ethelinda, who had not expected him to agree with her; 'the Lowther Arcade is not Regent Street.'

The jester did not care to dispute this. 'And were you very happy at Regent Street?' he asked.

'Happy?' she repeated. 'Well, I don't know; at least, one was not bored there. I was in the best set, you see, the two-guinea one, and they were always getting up something to amuse us in the window—a review, or a sham fight, or a garden-party, or something. Last winter they gave us a fancy-dress ball—I went as Mary Stuart, and was very much admired. But here—' and she finished the sentence with a disdainful little shrug.

'I don't think you'll find it so very bad here, when you get a little more used to it,' he said; 'our mistress—'

'Pray don't use that very unpleasant word,' she interrupted sharply. 'Did you never hear of "dolls' rights?" We call these people "hostesses."'

'Well, our hostess, then—Winifred, she's not unkind. She doesn't care much about me, and that cousin of hers, Master Archie, gives me a bad time of it when I come in his way, but really she's very polite and attentive to you.'

'Polite and attentive!' sneered Ethelinda (and if you have never seen a doll sneer, you can have no idea how alarming it is). 'I don't call it an attention to be treated like a baby by a little chit of a girl who can't dress herself properly yet—no style, no elegance, and actually a pinafore in the mornings!'

This is the way some of these costly lady dolls talk about their benefactresses when the gas is out and they think no one overhears them. I don't know whether the plain old-fashioned ones, who are not so carefully treated, but often more tenderly loved, are as bad; but it is impossible to say—dolls are exceedingly artful, and there are persons, quite clever in other things, who will tell you honestly that they do not understand them in the least.

'Then the society here,' Ethelinda went on, without much consideration for the other's feelings— perhaps she thought he was too cheap to have any—'it's really something too dreadful for words. Why, those people in the poky little house over there, with only four rooms and a front door they can't open, have never had the decency to call upon me. Not that I should take any notice, of course, if they did, but it just shows what they are. And the other day I actually overheard one frightful creature in a print dress, with nothing on her head but a great tin-tack, ask another horror "which she liked best—make-believe tea or orange-juice!"'

'Well, I prefer make-believe tea myself,' said the jester, 'because, you see, I can't get the orange-juice down, and so it's rather bad for the dress and complexion.'

'Possibly,' she said scornfully. 'I'm thankful to say I've not been called upon to try it myself—even Miss Winifred knows better than that. But, anyhow, it's horribly insipid here, and I suppose it will be like this always now. I did hope once that when I went out into the world I should be a heroine and have a romance of my own.'

'What is a romance?' he asked.

'I thought you wouldn't understand me,' she said; 'a romance is—well, there's champagne in it, and cigarettes, to begin with.'

'But what is champagne?' he interrupted.

'Something you drink,' she said; 'what else could it be?'

'I see,' he said; 'a sort of orange-juice.'

'Orange-juice!' Ethelinda cried contemptuously; 'it's not in the least like orange-juice; it's—' (she didn't know what it was made of herself, but there was no use in telling him so) 'I couldn't make you understand without too much trouble, you really are so very ignorant, but there's a good deal of it in romances. And dukes, and guardsmen, and being very beautiful and deliciously miserable, till just before the end—that's a romance! My milliner used to have it read out to her while she was dressing me for that ball I told you about.'

'Do you mind telling me what a heroine is?' he asked. 'I know I'm very stupid.'

'A heroine? oh, any doll can be a heroine. I felt all the time the heroines were all just like me. They were either very good or very wicked, and I'm sure I could be the one or the other if I got the chance. I think it would be more amusing, perhaps, to be a little wicked, but then it's not quite so easy, you know.'

'I should think it would be more uncomfortable,' he suggested.

'Ah, but then you see you haven't any sentiment about you,' she said disparagingly.

'No,' he admitted, 'I'm afraid I haven't. I suppose they couldn't put it in for elevenpence three farthings.'

'I should think not,' Ethelinda observed, 'it's very expensive.' And then, after a short silence, she said more confidentially, 'you were talking of Master Archie just now. I rather like that boy, do you know. I believe I could make something of him if he would only let me.'

'He's a mischievous boy,' said the jester, 'and ill-natured too.'

'Yes, isn't he?' she agreed admiringly; 'I like him for that. I fancy a duke or a guardsman must be something like him; they all had just his wicked black eyes and long restless fingers. It wouldn't be quite so dull if he would notice me a little; but he never will!'

'He's going back to school next week,' the jester said rather cheerfully.

'So soon!' sighed Ethelinda. 'There's hardly time for him to make a real heroine of me before that. How I wish he would! I shouldn't care how he did it, or what came of it. I'm sure I should enjoy it, and it would give me something to think about all my life.'

'Say that again, my dainty little lady; say it again!' cried a harsh, jeering voice from beside them, 'and, if you really mean it, perhaps the old Sausage-Glutton can manage it for you. He's done more wonderful things than that in his time, I can tell you.'

The voice came from an old German clock which stood on the mantelpiece, or rather, from a strange painted wooden figure which was part of it—an ugly old man, who sat on the top with a plate of sausages on his knees, and a fork in one hand. Every minute he slowly forked up a sausage from the plate to his mouth, and swallowed it suddenly, while his lower jaw wagged, and his narrow eyes rolled as it went down in a truly horrible manner.

The children had long since given him the name of 'Sausage-Glutton,' which he richly deserved. He was a sort of magician in his way, having so much clockwork in his inside, and he was spiteful and malicious, owing to the quantity of wooden sausages he bolted, which would have ruined anyone's digestion and temper.

'Good gracious!' cried Ethelinda, with a start, 'who is that person?'

'Somebody who can be a good kind friend to you, pretty lady, if you only give him leave. So you want some excitement here, do you? You want to be wicked, and interesting, and unfortunate, and all the rest of it, eh? And you'd like young Archibald (a nice boy that, by the way), you'd like him to give you a little romance? Well, then, he shall, and to-morrow too, hot and strong, if you like to say the word.'

Ethelinda was too much fluttered to speak at first, and she was a little afraid of the old man, too, for he leered all round in such an odd way, and ate so fast and jerkily.

'Don't—oh, please don't!' cried a little squeaky voice above him. It came from a queer little angular doll, with gold-paper wings, a spangled muslin dress, and a wand with a tinsel star at the end of it, who was fastened up on the wall above a picture. 'You won't like it—you won't, really!'

'Don't trust him,' whispered the jester; 'he's a bad old man; he ruined a very promising young dancing nigger only the other day, unhinged him so that he will never hook on any more.'

'Ha, ha!' laughed the Sausage-Glutton, as he disposed of another sausage, 'that old fellow in the peculiar coat is jealous, you know; he can't make a heroine of you, and so he doesn't want anyone else to. Who cares what he says? And as for our little wooden friend up above, well, I should hope a dainty duchess like you is not going to let herself be dictated to by a low jointed creature, who sets up for a fairy when she knows her sisters dance round white hats every Derby Day.'

'They're not sisters; they're second cousins,' squeaked the poor Dutch doll, very much hurt, 'and they don't mean any harm by it; it's only their high spirits. And whatever you say, I'm a fairy. I had a Christmas-tree of my own once; but I had to leave it, it was so expensive to keep up. Now, you take my advice, my dear, do,' she added to Ethelinda, 'don't you listen to him. He'd give all his sausages to see you in trouble, he would; but he can't do anything unless you give him leave.'

But of course it would have been a little too absurd if Ethelinda had taken advice from a flat-headed twopenny doll and a flabby jester from the Lowther Arcade. 'My good creatures,' she said to them, 'you mean well, no doubt, but pray leave this gentleman and me to settle our own affairs. Can you really get Master Archie to take some notice of me, sir?' she said to the figure on the clock.

'I can, my loveliest,' he said.

'And will it be exciting,' she asked, 'and romantic, and—and just the least bit wicked, too?'

'You shall be the very wickedest heroine in any nursery in the world,' he replied. 'Oh, dear me, how you will enjoy yourself!'

'Then I accept,' said Ethelinda; 'I put myself quite in your hands—I leave everything to you.'

'That's right!' cried the Sausage-Glutton, 'that's a brave little beauty. It's a bargain, then? To-morrow afternoon the fun will begin, and then—my springs and wheels—what a time you will have of it! He, he! You look out for Archibald!'

And then he trembled all over as the clock struck twelve, and went on eating his sausages without another word, while Ethelinda gave herself up to delightful anticipations of the wonderful adventures that were actually about to happen to her at last.

But the jester felt very uneasy about it all; he felt so sure that the old Sausage-Glutton's amiability had some trickery underneath it.

'You are a fairy, aren't you?' he said to the Dutch doll in a whisper; 'can't you do anything to help her?'

'No,' she said sulkily; 'and if I could, I wouldn't. She has chosen to put herself in his power, and whatever comes of it will serve her right. I don't know what he means to do, and I can't stop him. Still, if I can't help her, I can help you; and you may want it, because he is sure to be angry with you for trying to warn her.'

'But I never gave him leave to meddle with me,' said the jester.

'Have you got sawdust or bran inside you, or what?' asked the fairy.

'Neither,' he said; 'only the bellows I squeak with, and wire. But why?'

'I was afraid so. It's only the dolls with sawdust or bran inside them that he can't do whatever he likes with without their consent. He can do anything he chooses with you; but he shan't hurt you this time, if you only take care—for I'll grant you the very next thing you wish. Only do be careful now about wishing; don't be in a hurry and waste the wish. Wait till things are at their very worst.'

'Thank you very much,' he said; 'I don't mind for myself so much, but I should like to prevent any harm from coming to her. I'll remember.'

Then he bent towards Ethelinda and whispered: 'You didn't believe what the old man on the clock told you about me, did you? I'm not jealous—I'm only a poor jester, and you're a great lady. But you'll let me sit by you, and you'll talk to me sometimes in the evenings as you did to-night, won't you?'

But Ethelinda, though she heard him plainly, pretended to be fast asleep—it was of no consequence to her whether he was jealous or not.

Winifred was sitting the next afternoon alone in her nursery, trying to play. She was a dear little girl about nine years old, with long, soft, brown hair, a straight little nose, and brown eyes which just then had a wistful, dissatisfied look in them—for the fact was that, for some reason or other, she could not get on with her dolls at all.

The jester was not good-looking enough for her; they had put his eyes in so carelessly, and his face had such a 'queer' look, and he was altogether a limp, unmanageable person. She always said to herself that she liked him 'for the sake of the giver,' poor clumsy, good-hearted Martha, the housemaid, who had left in disgrace, and presented him as her parting gift; but one might as well not be cared for at all as be liked in that roundabout way.

And Ethelinda, beautiful and fashionable as she was, was not friendly, and Winifred never could get intimate with her; she felt afraid to treat her as a small child younger than herself, it seemed almost a liberty to nurse her, for Ethelinda seemed to be quite grown up and to know far more than she did herself.

She sat there looking at Ethelinda, and Ethelinda stared back at her in a cold, distant way, as if she half remembered meeting her somewhere before. There was a fixed smile on her vermilion lips which seemed false and even a little contemptuous to poor lonely little Winifred, who thought it was hard that her own doll should despise her.

The jester's smile was amiable enough, though it was rather meaningless, but then no one cared about him or how he smiled, as he lay unnoticed on his back in the corner.

You would not have guessed it from their faces, but both dolls were really very much excited; each was thinking about the Sausage-Glutton and his vague promises, and wondering if, and how, those promises were to be carried out.

The wooden magician himself was bolting his sausage a minute on the top of the clock just as usual, only the jester fancied his cunning eyes rolled round at them with a peculiar leer as a cheerful whistle was heard on the stairs outside.

A moment afterwards a lively brown-faced boy in sailor dress put his head in at the door. 'Hullo, Winnie,' he said, 'are you all alone?'

'Nurse has gone downstairs,' said Winnie, plaintively; 'I've got the dolls, but it's dull here somehow. Can't you come and help me to play, Archie?'

Archie had been skating all the morning, and could not settle down just then to any of his favourite books, so he had come up to see Winnie with the idea of finding something to amuse him there—for though he was a boy, he did unbend at times, so far as to help her in her games, out of which he managed to get a good deal of amusement in his own peculiar way.

But of course he had to make a favour of it, and must not let Winifred see that it was anything but a sacrifice for him to consent.

'I've got other things to do,' he said; 'and you know you always make a fuss when I do play with you. Look at last time!'

'Ah, but then you played at being a slave-driver, Archie, and you made me sell you my old black Dinah for a slave, and then you tied her up and whipped her. I didn't like that game! But if you'll stay this time, I won't mind what else you do!'

For Archie had a way of making the dolls go through exciting adventures, at which Winifred assisted with a fearful wonder that had a fascination about it.

'Girls don't know how to play with dolls, and that's a fact,' said Archie. 'I could get more fun out of that dolls' house than a dozen girls could' (he would have set fire to it); 'but I tell you what: if you'll let me do exactly what I like, and don't go interfering, except when I tell you to, perhaps I will stay a little while—not long, you know.'

'I promise,' said Winifred, 'if you won't break anything. I'll do just what you tell me.'

'Very well then, here goes; let's see who you've got. I say, who's this in the swell dress?'

He was pointing to Ethelinda, whose brain began to tingle at once with a delicious excitement. 'He has noticed me at last,' she thought; 'I wonder if I could make him fall desperately in love with me!' and she turned her big blue eyes full upon him. 'Ah, if I could only speak—but perhaps I shall presently. I'm quite sure the romance is going to begin!'

'That's Ethelinda, Archie—isn't she pretty?'

'I've seen them uglier,' he said; 'she's like that Eve de Something we saw at Drury Lane—we'll have her, and there's that chap in the fool's dress, we may want him. Now we're ready.'

'What are you going to do with them, Archie?'

'You leave that to me. I've an idea, something much better than your silly tea-parties.'

'Why doesn't he tell that child to go?' thought Ethelinda, 'we don't want her!'

'Now listen, Winifred,' said Archie: 'this is the game. You're a beautiful queen (only do sit up and take that finger out of your mouth—queens don't do that). Well, and I'm the king, and this is your maid of honour, the beautiful Lady Ethelinda, see?'

'Go on, Archie; I see,' cried Winifred; 'and I like it so far.'

'I think I ought to have been the queen!' said Ethelinda to herself.

'Well, now,' said the boy, 'I'll tell you something. This maid of honour of yours doesn't like you (don't say she does, now; I'm telling this, and I know). You watch her carefully. Can't you see a sort of look in her face as if she didn't think much of you?'

'How clever he is,' thought Ethelinda; 'he knows exactly how I feel!'

'Do you really think it's that, Archie?' said Winifred; 'it's just what I was afraid of before you came in.'

'That's it. Look out for a kind of glare in her eye when I pay you any attention. (How does Your Majesty do? Well, I hope.) There, didn't you see it? Well, that's jealousy, that is. She hates you like anything!'

'I'm sure she doesn't, then,' protested Winifred.

'Oh, well, if you know better than I do, you can finish it for yourself. I'm going.'

'No, no; do stay. I like it. I'll be good after this!'

'Don't you interrupt again, then. Now the real truth is that she'd like to be queen instead of you; she's ambitious, you know—that's what's the matter with her. And so she's got it into her head that if you were only out of the way, I should ask her to be the next queen!'

Winifred could not say a word, she was so overcome by the idea of her doll's unkindness; and Archie took Ethelinda by the waist and brought her near her royal mistress as he said: 'Now you'll see how artful she is; she's coming to ask you if she may go out. Listen. "Please, Your Gracious Majesty, may I go out for a little while?"'

'This is even better than if I spoke myself,' Ethelinda thought; 'he can talk for me, and I do believe I'm going to be quite wicked presently.'

'Am I to speak to her, Archie?' Winifred asked, feeling a little nervous.

'Of course you are. Go on; don't be silly; give her leave.'

'Certainly, Ethelinda, if you wish it,' replied Winifred, with a happy recollection of her mother's manner on somewhat similar occasions, 'but I should like you to be in to prayers.'

'A maid of honour isn't the same as a housemaid, you know,' said Archie; 'but never mind—she's off. You don't see where she goes, of course.'

'Yes I do,' said Winifred.

'Ah, but not in the game; nobody does. She goes to the apothecary's—here's the apothecary.' And he caught hold of the jester, who thought helplessly, 'I'm being brought into it now; I wish he'd let me alone—I don't like it!' 'Well, so she says, "Oh, if you please, Mr. Apothecary, I want some arsenic to kill the royal blackbeetles with; not much—a pound or two will be plenty." So he takes down a jar (here Archie got up and fetched a big bottle of citrate of magnesia from a cupboard), 'and he weighs it out, and wraps it up, and gives it to her. And he says, "You'll mind and be very careful with it, my lady. The dose is one pinch in a teaspoonful of treacle to each blackbeetle, the last thing at night; but it oughtn't to be left about in places." And so Lady Ethelinda takes it home and hides it.'

'I've bought some poison now,' thought Ethelinda, immensely delighted, 'I am a wicked doll! How convenient it is to have it all done for one like this! I do hope he's going to make me give Winifred some of that stuff, to get her out of the way, and have the romance all to our two selves.'

'Now you and I,' Archie continued, 'haven't the least idea of all this. But one day, the Court jester ('I was an apothecary just now,' thought the jester; 'it's really very confusing!')—the Court jester comes up, looking very grave, and sneaks of her. The reason of that is that he's angry with her because she never will have anything to do with him, and he says that he's seen her folding up a powder in paper and writing on it, and he thought I ought to be told about it.' ('This is awful,' thought the jester. 'What will Ethelinda think of me for telling tales? and what has come to Ethelinda? It's all that miserable Sausage-Glutton's doing—and I can't help myself!')

'Well, I'm very much surprised of course,' said Archie; 'any king would be—but I wait, and one day, when she has gone out for a holiday, the jester and I go to her desk and break it open.'

'Oh, Archie,' objected the poor little Queen in despair, 'isn't that rather mean of you?'

'Now look here, Winnie, I can't have this sort of thing every minute. For a gentleman, it might be rather mean, perhaps, but then I'm a king, and I've got a right to do it, and it's all for your sake, too—so you can't say anything. Besides, it's the jester does it; I only look on. Well, and by-and-by,' said Archie, as he scribbled something laboriously on a piece of paper, 'by-and-by he finds this!'

And with imposing gravity he handed Winifred a folded paper, on which she read with real terror and grief the alarming words—'Poisin for the Queen!'

'There, what do you think of that?' he asked triumphantly; 'looks bad, doesn't it?'

'Perhaps,' suggested the Queen feebly, 'perhaps it was only in fun?'

'Fun—there's not much fun about her! Now the guard' (here he used the bewildered jester once more) 'arrests her. Do you want to ask the prisoner any questions?—you can if you like.'

'You—you didn't mean to poison me really, did you, Ethelinda dear?' said Winifred, who was taking it all very seriously, as she took most things. 'Archie, do make her say something!'

'Why can't you answer when the Queen asks you a question, eh?' demanded Archie. 'No, she won't say a word; she'll only grin at you; you see she's quite hardened. There's only one thing that would make her confess,' he added cautiously, aware that he was on rather delicate ground, 'and that's the torture. I could make a beautiful rack, Winnie, if you didn't mind?'

'Whatever she's done,' said the Queen, firmly, 'I'm not going to have her tortured! And I believe she's sorry inside and wants me to forgive her!'

'Then why doesn't she say so?' said Archie. 'No, no, Winnie. Look here, this is a serious thing, you know; it won't do to pass it over; it's high treason, and she'll have to be tried.'

'But I don't want her tried,' said Winifred.

'Oh, very well then; I had better go downstairs again and read. The best part was all coming, but if you don't care, I'm sure I don't!'

'Little idiot!' thought Ethelinda angrily, 'she'll spoil the whole thing; every heroine has to be tried!'

But Winnie gave in, as she usually did, to Archie. 'Well, then, she shall be tried if you really think she ought to be, Archie; it won't hurt her though, will it?'

'Of course it won't; it's all right. Now for the trial: here's the court, and here's a place for the judge' (he built it all up with books and bricks as he spoke); 'here's the dock—stick Lady What's-her-name inside— that's it. We must do without a jury, but I suppose we ought to have a judge; oh, this fellow will do for judge!'

And he seized the jester and raised him to the Bench at once. The jester was more puzzled than ever. 'Now I'm a judge,' he thought, 'I shall have to try her; but I'm glad of it—I'll let her off!'

But unluckily he very soon found that he had no voice at all in the matter, except what Archie chose to lend him.

'Oh, but Archie,' said Winifred, who was determined to defeat the ends of justice if she possibly could, 'can a jester be a judge?'

'Why not?' said Archie; 'judges make jokes sometimes—I've heard papa say so, and he's a barrister, and ought to know.'

'But this one doesn't make real jokes!' persisted Winifred.

'Who asked him to? Judges are not obliged to make jokes, Winnie. I believe you are trying to get her off, but I'm going to see justice done, I tell you. So now then, Lady Ethelinda, you are charged with high treason and trying to poison Her Most Gracious Majesty, Queen Winifred Gladys Robertson, by putting arsenic in Her Majesty's tea. Guilty or not guilty! Speak up!'

'Not guilty!' put in Winifred quickly, thinking that would settle the whole trial comfortably. 'There, Archie, you can't say she didn't speak that time!'

'Now, you have done it!' Archie said triumphantly. 'If she'd confessed, we might have shown mercy. Now we shall have to prove it, and if we do I'm sorry for her, that's all!'

'If she says "Guilty, and she won't do it again!"' suggested Winifred.

'It's too late for that now,' said Archie, who was not going to have his trial cut short in that way: 'no, we must prove it.'

'But how are you going to prove it?'

'You wait. I've been in court once or twice with papa, and seen him prove all sorts of things. First, we must have in the fellow who sold the poison—the apothecary, you know. Oh, I say, though, I forgot that—he's the judge; that won't do!'

'Then you can't prove it after all—I'm so glad!' cried the Queen, with her eyes sparkling.

'One would think you rather liked being poisoned,' said Archie, in an offended tone.

'I like magnesia, and it isn't poison, really—it's medicine.'

'It isn't magnesia now; it's arsenic; and she shan't get off like this. I'll call the apothecary's young man, he'll prove it (this brick is the apothecary's young man). There, he says it's all right; she did it right enough. Now for the sentence! (put a penwiper on the judge's head, will you, Winnie; it's solemner).'

'What's a sentence?' asked Winifred, much disturbed at these ill-omened arrangements.

'You'll see; this is the judge talking now: "Lady Ethelinda, you've been found guilty of very bad conduct; you've put arsenic in your beloved Queen's tea!"'

'Why, I haven't had tea yet!' protested the Sovereign.

"Her Majesty is respectfully ordered not to interrupt the judge when he's summing up; it puts him out. Well, as I was saying, Lady Ethelinda, I'm sorry to tell you that we shall have to cut your head off!"'

'What have I done?' thought the jester; 'she'll think I'm in earnest; she'll never forgive me!'

But Ethelinda was perfectly delighted, for not one of her heroines had ever been in such a romantic position as this. 'And of course,' she thought, 'it will all come right in the end; it always does.'

Winifred, however, was terrified by the sternness of the court: 'Archie,' she cried, 'she mustn't have her head cut off.'

'It will be all right, Winnie, if you will only leave it to me and not interfere. You promised not to interrupt, and yet you will keep on doing it!'

Archie's head was full of executions just then, for he had been reading 'The Tower of London;' he had been artfully leading up to an execution from the very first, and he meant to have his own way.

But first he amused himself by working upon Winifred's feelings, which was a bad habit of his on these occasions. To do him justice, he did not know how keenly she felt things, and how soon she forgot it was only pretence; it flattered him to see how easily he could make Winifred cry about nothing, and he never guessed what real pain he was giving her.

'Winnie,' he began very dolefully, 'she's in prison now, languishing in her prison cell, and do you know, I rather think her heart's beginning to soften a little: she wants you to come and see her. You won't refuse her last request, Winnie, will you?'

'As if I could!' cried Winifred, full of the tenderest compassion.

'Very well then; this is the last meeting. "My dear kind mistress" (it's Ethelinda speaking to you now), "that I once loved so dearly in the happy days when I was innocent and good, I couldn't die till I had asked you to forgive me. Let your poor wicked maid-of-honour kiss your hand just once more as she used to do; tell her you forgive her about that arsenic." Now then, Winnie!'

'I—I can't, Archie!' sobbed Winifred, quite melted by this pathetic appeal.

'If you don't, she'll think you're angry still, and won't forgive her,' said Archie. 'Just you listen; this is her now: "Won't you say one little word, Your Majesty; you might as well. When I'm gone and mouldering away in my felon's grave it will be too late then, and you'll be sorry. It's the last thing I shall ever ask you!"'

'Oh, Ethelinda, darling, don't!' implored her Queen; 'don't go on talking in that dreadful way; I can't bear it. Archie, I must forgive her now!'

'Oh yes, forgive her,' he said with approval; 'queens shouldn't sulk or bear malice.'

'It's all right,' said Winifred briskly, as she dried her eyes; 'she's quite good again. Now let's play at something not quite so horrid!'

'When we've done with this, we will; but it isn't half over yet; there's all the execution to come. It's the fatal day now, the dismal scaffold is erected' (here he made a rough platform and a neat little block with the books), 'the sheriff is mounting guard over it' (and Archie propped up the unfortunate jester against a workbox so that he overlooked the scaffold); 'the trembling criminal is brought out amidst the groans of the populace (groan, Winnie, can't you?)'

'I shan't groan,' said Winnie, rebelliously; 'I'm a queen, not a populace. Archie, you won't really cut off her head, will you?'

'Don't be a little duffer,' said he; 'the end is to be a surprise, so I can't tell you what it is till it comes. You've heard of pardons arriving just in time, haven't you? Very well then. Only I don't say one will arrive here, you know, I only say, wait!'

'And now,' he went on, 'I'm not the King any longer, I'm the headsman; and—and I say, Winnie, perhaps you'd better hide your face now; a queen wouldn't look on at the execution, really; at least a nice queen wouldn't!'

So Winifred hid her face in her hands obediently, very glad to be spared even the pretence of an execution, and earnestly wishing Archie was near the end of this uncomfortable game.

But Archie was just beginning to enjoy himself: 'The wretched woman,' he announced with immense unction, 'is led tottering to the block, and then the headsman, very respectfully, cuts off some of her beautiful golden hair, so that it shouldn't get in his way.'

At this point I am sorry to say that Archie, in the wish to have everything as real as possible, actually did snip off a good part of Ethelinda's flossy curls. Luckily for him, his cousin was too conscientious and unsuspecting to peep through her fingers, and never imagined that the scissors she heard were really cutting anything—she even kept her eyes shut while Archie hunted about the room for something, which he found out at last, and which was a sword in a red tin scabbard.

Till then Archie was not quite sure what he really meant to do; at first he had fancied that it would be enough for him just to touch Ethelinda lightly with the sword, but now (whether the idea had been put in his head by the Sausage Glutton, or whether it had been there somewhere all the time) he began to think how easily the sharp blade would cleave Ethelinda's soft wax neck, and how he could hold up the severed head by the hair, just like the executioner in the pictures, and say solemnly, 'This is the head of a traitress!'

He knew of course that it would get him into terrible trouble, and he ought to have known that it would be mean and cowardly of him to take advantage of his poor little cousin's trust in him to deceive her.

But he did not stop to think of that; the temptation was too strong for him; he had gone so far in cutting off her hair that he might just as well cut off her head too.

So that presently Ethelinda found herself lying helpless, with her hands tied behind her, and her close-cropped head placed on a thick book, while Archie stood over her with a cruel gleam in his eyes, and flourished a flashing sword.

'I ought to be masked though,' he said suddenly, 'or I might be recognised—executioners had to be masked. I'll tie a handkerchief over my eyes and that will have to do.'

And when he had done this, he began to measure the distance with his eye, and to make some trial cuts to be quite sure of his aim, for he meant to get the utmost possible enjoyment out of it.

Ethelinda began to be terribly frightened. Being a heroine was not nearly so pleasant as she had expected. It had cost her most of her beautiful hair already: was it going to cost her her head as well?

Too late, she began to see how foolish she had been, and that even make-believe tea-parties were better than this. She longed to be held safe in tender-hearted little Winifred's arms.

But Winifred's eyes were shut tight, and would not be opened till—till all was over. Ethelinda could not move, could not cry out to her, she was quite helpless, and all the time the wicked old man on the clock went on steadily swallowing sausage after sausage, as if he had nothing at all to do with it!

The jester was even more alarmed for Ethelinda than she was herself; he was quite certain that Winifred was being wickedly deceived, and that the pardon so cunningly suggested would never come.

In another minute this dainty little lady, with the sweet blue eyes and disdainful smile, would be gone from him for ever; and there was no hope for her,—none!

And the bitterest thing about it was, that, although he was a great deal confused, as he very well might be, as to how it had all come about, he knew that in some way, he himself had taken part (or rather several parts) in bringing her to this shameful end, and the poor jester, innocent as he was, fancied that her big eyes had a calm scorn and reproach in them as she looked up at him sideways from the block.

'What shall I do without her?' he thought; 'how can I bear it. Ah, I ought to be lying there—not she. I wish I could take her place!'

All this time Archie had been lingering—he lingered so long that Winifred lost all patience. 'Do make haste, Archie,' she said, with a little shudder that shook the table. 'I can't bear it much longer; I shall have to open my eyes!'

'It was only the mask got in my way,' he said. 'Now I'm ready. One, two, three!'

And then there was a whistling swishing sound, followed by a heavy thud, and a flop.

After that Archie very prudently made for the door. 'I—I couldn't help it, really, Winnie,' he stammered, as she put her hands down with relief and looked about, rather dazzled at first by the sudden light. 'I'll save up and buy you another twice as pretty. And you know you said Ethelinda didn't seem to care about you!'

'Stop, Archie, what do you mean? Did you think you'd cut her head off really!'

'Haven't I?' said Archie, stupidly. 'I cut something's head off; I saw it go!'

'Then you did mean it! And, oh, it's the jester! I wouldn't have minded it so much, if you hadn't meant it for Ethelinda! And, Archie, you cruel, bad boy—you've cut—cut all her beautiful hair off, and I sat here and let you! She's not pretty at all now—it's a shame, it is a shame!'

Ethelinda had had a wonderful escape, and this is how it had happened:

The jester had been so anxious about Ethelinda that he had forgotten all about the fairy, and how she had granted him his very next wish; but she, being a fairy, had to remember it. If he had only thought of it, it would have been just as easy to wish Ethelinda safe without any harm coming to himself, but he had wished 'to take her place,' and the fairy, whether she liked it or not, was obliged to keep her promise.

So the little shake which Winifred had given the table was enough to make Ethelinda roll quietly over the edge of the platform, and the jester, who never was very firm on his legs, fall forward on his face the next moment, exactly where she had lain—and either the fairy or the handkerchief over his face prevented Archie from finding out the exchange in time.

Archie tried to defend himself: 'I think she looks better with her hair cut short,' he said; 'lots of girls wear it like that. And, don't you see, Winnie, this has been a plot got up by the jester; Ethelinda was innocent all the time, and he's just nicely caught in his own trap.... That—that's the surprise!'

'I don't believe you one bit!' said Winifred. 'You had no business to cut even my jester's head off, but you meant to do much worse! I won't play with you any more, and I shan't forgive you till the very day you go back to school!'

'But, Winnie,' protested Archie, looking rather sheepish and ashamed of himself.

'Go away directly,' said Winnie, stamping her foot; 'I don't want to listen; leave me alone!'

So Archie went, not sorry, now, that an accident had kept him from doing his worst, and feeling tolerably certain that he would be able to make his cousin relent long before the time she had fixed, while Winifred, left to herself again, was so absorbed in sobbing over Ethelinda's sad disfigurement, that she quite forgot to pick up the split halves of the jester's head which were lying on the nursery floor.

That night Ethelinda had the chest of drawers all to herself, and the old Sausage Glutton grinned savagely at her from the mantelpiece, for he was disappointed at the way in which his plans had turned out.

'Good evening,' he began, with one of his nastiest sneers. 'And how are you after your little romance, eh? Master Archie very nearly had your pretty little empty head off—but of course I couldn't allow that. I hope you enjoyed yourself?'

'I did at first,' said Ethelinda; 'I got frightened afterwards, when I thought it wasn't going to end at all nicely. But did you notice how very wickedly that dreadful jester behaved to me—it will be a warning to me against associating with such persons in future, and I assure you that there was something about him that made me shudder from the very first! I have heard terrible things about the dolls in the Lowther Arcade, and what can you expect at such prices? Well, he's rewarded for his crimes, and that's a comfort to think of—but it has all upset me very much indeed, and I don't want any more romance—it does shorten the hair so!'

The Dutch fairy doll heard her and was very angry, for she knew of course why the jester had come to a tragic ending.

'Shall I tell her now, and make her ashamed and sorry—would she believe me? would she care? Perhaps not, but I must speak out some time—only I had better wait till the clock has stopped. I can't bear her to talk about that poor jester in this way.'

But it really did not matter to the jester, who could hear or feel nothing any more—for they had thrown him into the dustbin, where, unless the dustcart has called since, he is lying still.


## AN UNDERGRADUATE'S AUNT

Francis Flushington belonged to a small college, and by becoming a member conferred upon it one of the few distinctions it could boast—the possession of the very bashfulest man in the whole university.

But his college did not treat him with any excess of adulation on that account, and, probably from a prudent fear of rubbing the bloom off his modesty, allowed him to blush unseen—which was indeed the condition in which he preferred to blush.

He felt himself distressed in the presence of his fellow men, by a dearth of ideas and a difficulty in knowing which way to look, that made him happiest when he had fastened his outer door, and secured himself from all possibility of intrusion—although this was almost an unnecessary precaution on his part, for nobody ever thought of coming to see Flushington.

In appearance he was a man of middle height, with a long neck and a large head, which gave him the air of being shorter than he really was; he had little weak eyes which were always blinking, a nose and mouth of no particular shape, and hair of no definite colour, which he wore long—not because he thought it becoming, but because he hated having to talk to his hairdresser.

He had a timid deprecating manner, due to the consciousness that he was an uninteresting anomaly, and he certainly was as impervious to the ordinary influences of his surroundings as any modern under-graduate could well be.

Flushington had never particularly wanted to be sent to Cambridge, and when he was there he did not enjoy it, and had not the faintest hope of distinguishing himself in anything; he lived a colourless, aimless sort of life in his little sloping rooms under the roof where he read every morning from nine till two with a superstitious regularity, even when his books failed to convey any ideas whatever to his brain, which was not a remarkably powerful organ.

If the afternoon was fine, he generally sought out his one friend, who was a shade less shy than himself, and they went a monosyllabic walk together (for of course Flushington did not row, or take up athletics in any form); if it was wet, he read the papers and magazines at the Union, and in the evenings after hall, he studied 'general literature'—a graceful periphrasis for novels—or laboriously picked out a sonata or a nocturne upon his piano, a habit which had not tended to increase his popularity.

Fortunately for Flushington, he had no gyp, or his life would have been a burden to him, and with his bedmaker he was rather a favourite, as a 'gentleman what gave no trouble'—which meant that when he observed his sherry sinking like the water in a lock when the sluices are up, he was too delicate to refer to the phenomenon in any way.

One afternoon when Flushington was engaged over his modest luncheon of bread and butter, potted meat, and lemonade, he suddenly became aware of a sound of unusual voices and a strange flutter of female dresses on the winding stone staircase outside—and was instantly overcome with a cold dread.

Now, although there were certainly ladies coming upstairs, there was no reason for alarm; they were probably friends of the man who kept opposite, and was always having his people up. But Flushington had one of those odd presentiments, so familiar to nervous persons, that something unpleasant was at hand; he could not imagine who these ladies might be, but he knew instinctively that they were coming to him!

If he could only be sure that his outer oak was safely latched! He rose from his chair with wild ideas of rushing to see, of retreating to his bedroom, and hiding under the bed until they had gone.

Too late! the dresses were rustling now in his very passage; there was a pause evidently before his inner door, a few faint and smothered laughs, some little feminine coughs, then—two taps.

Flushington stood still for a moment, feeling like a caged animal; he had thoughts, even then, of concealment—was there time to get under the sofa? No, it would be too dreadful if the visitors, whoever they were, were to discover him in so unusual a situation.

So he ran back to his chair and sat down before crying 'Come in' in a faint voice. He did wish he had been reading anything but the work of M. Zola, which was propped up in front of him, but there was no time to put it away.

Your mild man often has a taste for seeing the less reputable side of life in a safe and second-hand way, and Flushington would toil manfully through the most realistic descriptions without turning a hair; now and then he looked out a word in the dictionary, and when it was not to be found there—and it generally wasn't—he had a sense almost of injury. But there was a strong fascination for him in experiencing the sensation of a kind of intellectual orgie, for he knew enough of the language to be aware that the incidents frequently bordered on the improper, even while it was not exactly clear in what the impropriety consisted.

As he said 'Come in,' the door opened, and his heart seemed to stop, and all the blood in it rushed violently up to his head, as a large lady came sweeping in, her face rippling with a broad smile of affection.

She horrified Flushington, who knew nobody with the smallest claim to smile at him so expansively as that, and he drank lemonade to conceal his confusion.

'You don't know me, my dear Frank,' she said easily; 'why of course you don't; how should you? Well, I'm (for goodness sake, my dear boy, don't look so dreadfully frightened, I don't want to eat you!) I'm your aunt—your Aunt Amelia, you know me now—from Australia, you know!'

This was a severe shock to Flushington, who had not even known he possessed such a relative anywhere; all he could say just then was, 'Oh, are you?' which he felt at the time was not quite the welcome to give an aunt who had come all the way from the Antipodes.

'Yes, that I am!' she said cheerily, 'but that's not all. I've another surprise for you—the dear girls would insist upon coming up too, to see their grand college cousin; they're just outside. I'll call them in, shall I?'

And in another second Flushington's small room was overrun by a horde of female relatives, while he could only look on and gasp.

They were pretty girls too, most of them, but that only frightened him more; he did not mind plain women half so much; some of them looked bright and clever as well, and a combination of beauty and intellect always reduced him to a condition of hopeless imbecility.

He had never forgotten one occasion on which he had been captured and introduced to a charming young lady from Newnham, and all he could do was to back feebly into a corner, murmuring 'Thank you' repeatedly.

He showed himself to scarcely more advantage now, as his aunt proceeded to single out one girl after another. 'We needn't have any formal nonsense between cousins,' she said; 'you know all their names already, I dare say. This is Milly, and that's Jane; and here's Flora, and Kitty, and Margaret, and this is my little Thomasina, keeping close to mamma, as usual.'

Poor Flushington ducked blindly in the various directions at the mention of each name, and then collectively to all; he had not sufficient presence of mind to offer them chairs, or cake, or anything, and besides, there was not nearly enough for that multitude.

Meanwhile his aunt had spread herself comfortably out in his only arm-chair, and was untying her bonnet-strings, while she beamed at him until he was ready to expire with embarrassment. 'I do think, Frankie dear,' she observed at last, 'that when an old auntie all the way from Australia takes the trouble to come and see you like this, the least—the very least you could do would be to give her one little kiss.'

She seemed so hurt by the omission, that Flushington dared not refuse; he staggered up and kissed her somewhere upon her face—after which he did not know which way to look, so terribly afraid was he that the same ceremony might have to be gone through with all the cousins, and he could not have survived that.

Happily for him, however, they did not appear to expect it, and he balanced a chair on its hind legs and, resting one knee upon it, waited for them to begin a conversation, for he could not think of a single apposite remark himself.

His aunt came to his rescue. 'You don't ask after your Uncle Samuel—have you forgotten all the beetles and things he used to send you?' she said reprovingly.

'No,' said Flushington, to whom Uncle Samuel was another revelation. 'How is the beetle—I mean, how is Uncle Samuel? Quite well, I hope?'

'Only tolerably so, Frank, thank you; as well as could be expected after his loss.'

'I didn't hear of that,' said Flushington, catching at this conversational rope in despair. 'Was it—did he lose much?'

'I was not referring to a money loss,' she said, and her glance was stony for the moment; 'I was (as I think you might have guessed) referring to the death of your cousin John.'

And Flushington, who had begun to feel his first agonies abating, had a terrible relapse at this unhappy mistake; he stammered something about it being very sad indeed, and then, wondering why no one had ever kept him better posted as to his relations, he resolved that he would not betray his ignorance by any further inquiries.

But his aunt was evidently wounded afresh. 'I ought to have known,' she said, and shook her head pathetically; 'they soon forget us when we leave the old country—and yet I did think, too, my own sister's son would remember his cousin's death! Well, well, my loves, we must teach him to know us better now we have the opportunity. Frankie dear, the girls and I expect you to take us about everywhere and show us all the sights; or what's the use of having a nephew at Cambridge University, you know.'

Flushington had a horrible mental vision of himself careering all over Cambridge at the head of a long procession of female relatives, a fearful prospect for so shy a man. 'Shall you be here long?' he asked.

'Oh, only a week or so; we're at the "Bull," very near you; and so we can always be popping in on you. And now, Frankie, my boy, will you think your aunt a very bold beggar if she asks you to give us a little something to eat? We wouldn't wait for lunch, the dear children were so impatient, and we're all ravenous! We all thought, the girls and I (didn't you, dears?) that it would be such fun lunching with a real college student in his own room.'

'Oh,' protested Flushington, 'I assure you there's nothing so extraordinary in it, and—and the fact is, I'm afraid there's very little for you to eat, and the kitchens and the buttery are closed by this time.' He said this at a venture, for he felt quite unequal to facing the college cook and ordering lunch from that tremendous personage—he would far rather order it from his tutor even.

'But,' he added, touched by the little cry of disappointment which the girls made in spite of themselves, 'if you don't mind potted ham—there's some left in the bottom of this tin, and there's some bread and an inch of butter, and a little marmalade and a few milk biscuits—and there was some sherry this morning!'

His cousins declared merrily that they were so hungry they would enjoy anything, and so they sat round the table and poor Flushington served out meagre rations to them of all the provisions he could hunt up, even to his figs and his French plums. It was like a shipwreck, he thought drearily. There was not nearly enough to go round, and they lunched with evident disillusionment, thinking that the college luxury of which they had heard so much had been sadly exaggerated.

During the meal the aunt began to study Flushington's features with affectionate interest. 'There's a strong look of poor dear Simon about him when he smiles,' she said, looking at him through her gold double-glasses. 'There, did you catch it, girls? Just his mother's profile! Turn your face a leetle more to the window; I want to get the light on your nose, Frankie; now don't you see the likeness to your aunt's portrait at Gumtree Creek, girls?'

And Flushington had to sit still with all the girls' charming eyes fixed critically upon his crimson countenance, until he would have given worlds to be able to slide down under the table and evade them, but of course he was obliged to remain above.

'He's got dear Caroline's nose!' the aunt announced triumphantly, and the cousins were agreed that he certainly had Caroline's nose—which made him feel vaguely that he ought at least to offer to return it.

Presently the youngest and prettiest of the girls whispered to her mother, who laughed indulgently. 'Why, you baby,' she said, 'what do you think this silly child wants me to ask you, Frankie? She says she would so like to see how you look in your college robes and that odd four-cornered hat you all wear. Will you put them on, just to please her?'

And he had to put them on and walk slowly up and down the room in his cap and gown, feeling all the time that he was making a dismal display of himself, and that the girls were plainly disappointed, for they admitted that somehow they had fancied the academical costume would have been more becoming.

After this came a hotly-sustained catechism upon his studies, his amusements, his friends, and his mode of life generally, and the aunt—who by this time felt the potted ham beginning to disagree with her— seemed to be unfavourably impressed by the answers she obtained.

This was particularly the case when to the question 'what church he attended,' he replied that he attended none, as he was always regular at chapel: for the aunt was disappointed to find her nephew a Dissenter, and said as much; while Flushington, though he saw the misunderstanding, was far too shy and too miserable to explain it.

The cousins by this time were clustered together, whispering and laughing over little private jokes, and he, after the manner of sensitive men, of course concluded they were laughing at him, and perhaps on this occasion he was not mistaken.

He stood by the fireplace, growing hotter and hotter every second, inwardly cursing his whole race, and wishing that his father had been a foundling. What would he have to do next? take all his people out for a walk. He trembled at the idea. He would have to pass through the court with them, under the eyes of the men who were loitering about the grass plots before going down to the boats; through the open window he could hear their voices, and the clash they made as they fenced with walking-sticks.

As he stood there, dumb and miserable, he heard another tap at his door—a feeble one this time.

'Why,' cried his aunt, 'that must be poor old Sophy at last—you may not remember old Sophy, Frankie; you were quite a baby when she came out to us; but she remembers you, and begged so hard to be allowed to come and see you. Don't keep her standing outside. Come in, Sophy; it's quite right; Master Frankie is here!'

And at this a very old person in a black bonnet came in, and was overcome by emotion at the first sight of Flushington. 'To think,' she quavered, 'to think as my dim old eyes should live to see the child I've dandled times and again on my lap growed out into a college gentleman!' Whereupon she hugged Flushington respectfully, and wept copiously upon his shoulder, which made him almost cataleptic.

But as she grew calmer, she became more critical, even confessing a certain feeling of disappointment with Flushington. He had not filled out, she declared, so fine as he'd promised to fill out. And when she began to drag up reminiscences of his early youth, asking if he recollected how he wouldn't be washed unless they first put his little spotted wooden horse on the washstand, and how they had to bribe him with a penny trumpet to take his castor oil, and how fond he used to be of senna tea, Flushington felt that he must seem more of a fool than ever!

This was quite bad enough, but at last the girls began to be restless, and there being no efforts made to entertain them, amused themselves by exploring their cousin's rooms and exclaiming at everything they saw; admiring his pipes and his umbrella rack, his buffalo horns and his tin heraldic shields, and his quaint wooden kettle-holder, until they came round to his French novel, and, as they were healthy-minded Colonial girls, with a limited knowledge of Parisian literature, they pounced upon it directly, and wanted Flushington to tell them what it was all about.

'Yes, Frankie, tell us,' the aunt struck in as he faltered; 'I'm always glad for the girls to know of any nice foreign works, as they've really improved wonderfully in their French lately.'

There are French novels, no doubt, of which it would be practicable and pleasant to give a general idea to one's aunt, but they are not numerous, and this particular book did not chance to be one of them.

So this demand threw him into a cold perspiration; he had not presence of mind to prevaricate or invent, and he would probably have committed himself in some deplorable manner, if just at that moment there had not happened to come another tap at the door, or rather a sharp rattle, as if with the end of something wooden.

Flushington's head swam with horror at this third interruption; he was prepared for anything now—another aunt, say from Greenland's icy mountains, or India's coral strand, with a fresh relay of female cousins, or a staff of aged family retainers who had washed him in early infancy: he sat there cowering.

But when the door opened, a tall, fair, good-looking young fellow in a boating-straw and flannels, and carrying a tennis racket, burst impulsively in. 'Oh, I say,' he began, 'you don't happen to have heard or seen anything of—oh, beg pardon, didn't see, you know,' he added, as he noticed the extraordinary fact that Flushington had people up.

'Oh—er—let me introduce you,' said Flushington, with a vague notion that this was the right thing to do; 'Mr. Lushington—Mrs. (no, I don't know her name)—my aunt ... my cousins!'

The young man, who had just been about to retire, bowed and stared with sudden surprise. 'Do you know,' he said slowly in an undertone to the other, 'do you know that I can't help fancying there's some mistake—are you sure that's not my aunt you've got hold of there?'

'Oh,' whispered Flushington, catching at this unexpected hope, 'do you really think so? She seems so certain she belongs to me!'

'Well,' said the new-comer, 'I only know I have an aunt and cousins I've never seen who were coming up some time this week—do these ladies happen to come from the Colonies, by the way?'

'Yes, yes!' cried Flushington, eagerly; 'it's all right, they belong to you; and, I say, do take them away; I can't bear it any longer!'

'Now, now, what's this whispering, Frankie?' cried the aunt; 'not very polite, I must say!'

'He says,' explained Flushington, 'he says it's all a mistake, and—and you're not my aunt at all!'

'Oh, indeed, does he?' she replied, drawing herself together with dignity; 'and may I ask who is this gentleman who knows so much about our family—I didn't catch the name?'

'My name is Lushington—Frank Lushington,' he said.

'Then—who are you?' she demanded, turning upon the unfortunate owner of the rooms; 'answer me, I insist upon it!'

'Me?' he stammered, 'I'm Francis Flushington. I—I'm very sorry—but I can't help it!'

'Why—why—then you're no nephew of mine, sir!' cried the aunt.

'Thank you very much,' said Flushington, with positive gratitude.

'But,' she said, 'I want to know why I have been allowed to deceive myself in this way. Perhaps, sir, you will kindly explain?'

'What's the good of asking me?' protested Flushington; 'I haven't an idea why!'

'I think I see,' put in her genuine nephew; 'you see, there isn't much light on the staircase outside, and you must have taken the "Flushington" over his oak to be "F. Lushington," and gone straight in, you know. They told me at the lodge that some ladies had been asking for me, and so when I didn't find you in my rooms, I thought I'd look in here on the chance—and here you all are, eh?'

But the aunt was annoyed to find that she had been pouring out all her pent-up affection over a perfect stranger, and had eaten his lunch into the bargain. She almost feared she had put herself in a slightly ridiculous position, and this, of course, made her feel very angry with Flushington.

'Yes, yes, yes!' she said excitedly, 'that's all very well; but why did he deliberately encourage me in my mistake?'

'How was I to know it was a mistake?' pleaded Flushington. 'You told me you were my aunt from Australia; for all I know Australia may be overrun with my aunts. I supposed you knew best.'

'But you asked affectionately after Samuel,' she persisted; 'you must have had some object in humouring my mistake.'

'You told me to ask after him, and I did,' said Flushington; 'what else could I do?'

'No, sir,' she said, rising in her wrath; 'it was a most ungentlemanly and heartless practical joke on your part, and—and I shall not listen to further excuses.'

'Oh, good gracious!' Flushington almost whimpered; 'a practical joke! me, oh, it really is too bad!'

'My dear aunt,' Lushington assured her, 'he's quite incapable of such a thing; it's a mistake on both sides; he wouldn't wish to intercept another fellow's aunt.'

'I wouldn't do such a thing for worlds!' protested Flushington, sincerely enough; he would not have robbed a fellow creature of a single relation of the remotest degree; and as for carrying off an aunt and a complete set of female cousins, he would have blushed (and, in fact, did blush) at the bare suspicion.

The cousins themselves had been laughing and whispering together all this time, regarding their new relation with shy admiration, very different from the manner in which they had looked at poor Flushington; the old nurse, too, was overjoyed at the exchange, and now declared that from the minute she set eyes on Flushington, she had felt something inside tell her that her Master Frank would never have turned out so undersized as him!

'Well,' said the aunt, mollified at last, 'you must forgive us for having disturbed you like this, Mr. a— Flushington' (the unfortunate man murmured that he did not mind it now); 'and now, Frank, my boy, I should like the girls to see your rooms.'

'Come along then,' said he. 'Will you let me give you something to eat?—I'll run down and see what they can let me have; and perhaps you'll kindly help me to lay the cloth; I never can lay the thing straight myself, and my old bedmaker's out of the way, as usual.'

The girls looked dubiously at one another—they were frightfully hungry still; at last the eldest, out of pure consideration for Flushington's feelings, said, 'Thank you very much, Cousin Frank—but your friend has kindly given us some lunch already.'

'Oh!' he said, 'has he though? That's really uncommonly good of you, old chap.'

But Flushington's modesty did not allow him to accept undeserved gratitude. 'I say,' he whispered, taking the other aside, 'I gave them what I could, but I'm afraid it—it wasn't much of a lunch.'

Lushington made a mental note that he would repeat his invitation when he had got his cousins outside. 'Well, look here,' he said, 'will you come and help me to row the ladies up to Byron's Pool—say in an hour from this—and we'll all come back and have a little dinner in my rooms, eh?'

'Yes, Mr. Flushington, do—do come,' the girls all entreated him, 'just to show you forgive us for taking possession of you like this.'

But Flushington wriggled out of it somehow. He couldn't come, he said uncomfortably; he had an engagement. He had nothing of the kind, but he felt that he had had quite enough female society for one day.

They did not press him, and he was heartily glad when the last of his temporary relations had filed out of his little room, leaving him reminiscences of a terrible half-hour which caused him to be extremely careful for months after not to lunch without ascertaining previously that his outer door was securely sported. But never again did a solitary hungry aunt invade his solitude.


## THE SIREN

Long long ago, a siren lived all alone upon a rocky little island far out in the Southern Ocean. She may have been the youngest and most beautiful of the original three sirens, driven by her sisters' jealousy, or her own weariness of their society, to seek this distant home; or she may have lived there in solitude from the beginning.

But she was not unhappy; all she cared about was the admiration and worship of mortal men, and these were hers whenever she wished, for she had only to sing, and her exquisite voice would float away over the waters, until it reached some passing vessel, and then every one that heard was seized instantly with the irresistible longing to hasten to her isle and throw himself adoringly at her feet.

One day as she sat upon a low headland, looking earnestly out over the sparkling blue-green water before her, and hoping to discover the peak of some far-off sail on the hazy sea-line, she was startled by a sound she had never heard before—the grating of a boat's keel on the pebbles in the little creek at her side.

She had been too much absorbed in watching for distant ships to notice that a small bark had been gliding round the other side of her island, but now, as she glanced round, she saw that the stranger who had guided it was already jumping ashore and securing his boat.

Evidently she had not attracted him there, for she had been too indolent to sing of late, and he did not seem even to have seen her, or to have landed from any other motive than curiosity.

He was quite young, gallant-looking and sunburnt, with brown hair curling over his forehead, an open face and honest grey eyes. And as she looked at him, the fancy came to her that she would like to question him and hear his voice; she would find out, if she could, what manner of beings these mortals were over whom she possessed so strange a power.

Never before had such a thought entered her mind, notwithstanding that she had seen many mortals of every age and rank, from captain to the lowest galley slave; but then she had only seen them under the influence of her magical voice, when they were struck dumb and motionless, after which—except as proofs of her power—they did not interest her.

But this stranger was still free—so long as she did not choose to enslave him; and for some reason she did not choose to do so just yet.

As he turned towards her, she beckoned to him imperiously, and he saw the slender graceful figure above for the first time,—the fairest maiden his eyes had ever beheld, with an unearthly beauty in her wonderful dark blue eyes, and hair of the sunniest gold,—he stood gazing at her in motionless uncertainty, for he thought he must be cheated by a vision.

He came nearer, and, obeying a careless motion of her hand, threw himself down on a broad shelf of rock a little below the spot where she was seated; still he did not dare to speak lest the vision should pass away.

She looked at him for some time with an innocent, almost childish, curiosity shining under her long lashes. At last she gave a low little laugh: 'Are you afraid of me?' she asked; 'why don't you speak? but perhaps,' she added to herself, 'mortals cannot speak.'

'I was silent,' he said, 'lest by speaking I should anger you—for surely you must be some goddess or sea-nymph?'

'Ah, you can speak!' she cried. 'No, I am no goddess or nymph, and you will not anger me—if only you will tell me many things I want to know!'

And she began to ask him all the questions she could think of: first about the great world in which men lived, and then about himself, for she was very curious, in a charmingly wilful and capricious fashion of her own.

He answered frankly and simply, but it seemed as if some influence were upon him which kept him from being dazzled and overcome by her loveliness, for he gave no sign as yet of yielding to the glamour she cast upon all other men, nor did his eyes gleam with the despairing adoration the siren knew so well.

She was quick to perceive this, and it piqued her. She paid less and less attention to the answers he gave her, and ceased at last to question him further.

Presently she said, with a strange smile that showed her cruel little teeth gleaming between her scarlet lips, 'Why don't you ask me who I am, and what I am doing here alone? do not you care to know?'

'If you will deign to tell me,' he said.

'Then I will tell you,' she said; 'I am a siren—are you not afraid now?'

'Why should I be afraid?' he asked, for the name had no meaning in his ears.

She was disappointed; it was only her voice—nothing else, then—that deprived men of their senses; perhaps this youth was proof even against that; she longed to try, and yet she hesitated still.

'Then you have never heard of me,' she said; 'you don't know why I sit and watch for the great gilded ships you mortals build for yourselves?'

'For your pleasure, I suppose,' he answered. 'I have watched them myself many a time; they are grand as they sweep by, with their sharp brazen beaks cleaving the frothing water, and their painted sails curving out firm against the sky. It is good to hear the measured thud of the great oars and the cheerful cries of the sailors as they clamber about the cordage.'

She laughed disdainfully. 'And you think I care for all that!' she cried. 'Where is the pleasure of looking idly on and admiring?—that is for them, not for me. As these galleys of yours pass, I sing—and when the sailors hear, they must come to me. Man after man leaps eagerly into the sea, and makes for the shore—until at last the oars grind and lock together, and the great ship drifts helplessly on, empty and aimless. I like that.'

'But the men?' he asked, with an uneasy wonder at her words.

'Oh, they reach the shore—some of them, and then they lie at my feet, just as you are lying now, and I sing on, and as they listen they lose all power or wish to move, nor have I ever heard them speak as you speak; they only lie there upon the sand or rock, and gaze at me always, and soon their cheeks grow hollower and hollower, and their eyes brighter and brighter—and it is I who make them so!'

'But I see them not,' said the youth, divided between hope and fear; 'the beach is bare; where, then, are all those gone who have lain here?'

'I cannot say,' she replied carelessly; 'they are not here for long; when the sea comes up it carries them away.'

'And you do not care!' he cried, struck with horror at the absolute indifference in her face; 'you do not even try to keep them here?'

'Why should I care?' said the siren lightly; 'I do not want them. More will always come when I wish. And it is so wearisome always to see the same faces, that I am glad when they go.'

'I will not believe it, siren,' groaned the young man, turning from her in bitter anguish; 'oh, you cannot be cruel!'

'No, I am not cruel,' she said in surprise. 'And why will you not believe me? It is true!'

'Listen to me,' he said passionately: 'do you know how bitter it is to die,—to leave the sunlight and the warm air, the fair land and the changing sea?'

'How can I know?' said the siren. 'I shall never die—unless—unless something happens which will never be!'

'You will live on, to bring this bitterness upon others for your sport. We mortals lead but short lives, and life, even spent in sorrow, is sweet to most of us; and our deaths when they come bring mourning to those who cared for us and are left behind. But you lure men to this isle, and look on unmoved as they are borne away!'

'No, you are wrong,' she said; 'I am not cruel, as you think me; when they are no longer pleasant to look at, I leave them. I never see them borne away. I never thought what became of them at last. Where are they now?'

'They are dead, siren,' he said sadly, 'drowned. Life was dear to them; far away there were women and children to whom they had hoped to return, and who have waited and wept for them since. Happy years were before them, and to some at least—but for you—a restful and honoured old age. But you called them, and as they lay here the greedy waves came up, dashed them from these rocks and sucked them, blinded, suffocating, battling painfully for breath and life, down into the dark green depths. And now their bones lie tangled in the sea-weed, but they themselves are wandering, sad, restless shades, in the shadowy world below, where is no sun, no happiness, no hope—but only sighing evermore, and the memory of the past!'

She listened with drooping lids, and her chin resting upon her soft palm; at last she said with a slight quiver in her voice,'I did not know—I did not mean them to die. And what can I do? I cannot keep back the sea.'

'You can let them sail by unharmed,' he said.

'I cannot!' she cried. 'Of what use is my power to me if I may not exercise it? Why do you tell me of men's sufferings—what are they to me?'

'They give you their lives,' he said; 'you fill them with a hopeless love and they die for it in misery—yet you cannot even pity them!'

'Is it love that brings them here?' she said eagerly. 'What is this that is called love? For I have always known that if I ever love—but then only—I must die, though what love may be I know not. Tell me, so that I may avoid it!'

'You need not fear, siren,' he said, 'for, if death is only to come to you through love, you will never die!'

'Still, I want to know,' she insisted; 'tell me!'

'If a stranger were to come some day to this isle, and when his eyes meet yours, you feel your indifference leaving you, so that you have no heart to see him lie ignobly at your feet, and cannot leave him to perish miserably in the cold waters; if you desire to keep him by your side—not as your slave and victim, but as your companion, your equal, for evermore—that will be love!'

'If that is love,' she cried joyously, 'I shall indeed never die! But that is not how men love me?' she added.

'No,' he said; 'their love for you must be some strange and enslaving passion, since they will submit to death if only they may hear your voice. That is not true love, but a fatal madness.'

'But if mortals feel love for one another,' she asked,'they must die, must they not?'

'The love of a man for a maiden who is gentle and good does not kill—even when it is most hopeless,' he said; 'and where she feels it in return, it is well for both, for their lives will flow on together in peace and happiness.'

He had spoken softly, with a far away look in his eyes that did not escape the siren.

'And you love one of your mortal maidens like that?' she asked. 'Is she more beautiful than I am?'

'She is mortal,' he said, 'but she is fair and gracious, my maiden; and it is she who has my love, and will have it while I live.'

'And yet,' she said, with a mocking smile, 'I could make you forget her.'

Her childlike waywardness had left her as she spoke the words, and a dangerous fire was shining in her deep eyes.

'Never!' he cried; 'even you cannot make me false to my love! And yet,' he added quickly, 'I dare not challenge you, enchantress that you are; what is my will against your power?'

'You do not love me yet,' she said; 'you have called me cruel, and reproached me; you have dared to tell me of a maiden compared with whom I am nothing! You shall be punished. I will have you for my own, like the others!'

'Siren,' he pleaded, seizing one of her hands as it lay close to him on the hot grey rock, 'take my life if you will—but do not drive away the memory of my love; let me die, if I must die, faithful to her; for what am I, or what is my love, to you?'

'Nothing,' she said scornfully, and yet with something of a caress in her tone, 'yet I want you; you shall lie here, and hold my hand, and look into my eyes, and forget all else but me.'

'Let me go,' he cried, rising, and turning back to regain his bark; 'I choose life while I may!'

She laughed. 'You have no choice,' she said; 'you are mine!' she seemed to have grown still more radiantly, dazzlingly fair, and presently, as the stranger made his way to the creek where his boat was lying, she broke into the low soft chant whose subtle witchery no mortals had ever resisted as yet.

He started as he heard her, but still he went on over the rocks a little longer, until at last he stopped with a groan, and turned slowly back; his love across the sea was fading fast from his memory; he felt no desire to escape any longer; he was even eager at last to be back on the ledge at her feet and listen to her for ever.

He reached it and sank down with a sigh, and a drowsy delicious languor stole over him, taking away all power to stir or speak.

Her song was triumphant and mocking, and yet strangely tender at times, thrilling him as he heard it, but her eyes only rested now and then, and always indifferently, upon his upturned face.

He wished for nothing better now than to lie there, following the flashing of her supple hands upon the harp-strings and watching every change of her fair face. What though the waves might rise round him and sweep him away out of sight, and drown her voice with the roar and swirl of waters? it would not be just yet.

And the siren sang on; at first with a cruel pride at finding her power supreme, and this youth, for all his fidelity, no wiser than the rest; he would waste there with yearning, hopeless passion, till the sight of him would weary her, and she would leave him to drift away and drown forgotten.

Yet she did not despise him as she had despised all the others; in her fancy his eyes bore a sad reproach, and she could look at him no longer with indifference.

Meanwhile the waves came rolling in fast, till they licked the foot of the rock, and as the foam creamed over the shingle, the siren found herself thinking of the fate which was before him, and, as she thought, her heart was wrung with a new strange pity.

She did not want him to be drowned; she would like him there always at her feet, with that rapt devotion upon his face; she almost longed to hear his voice again—but that could never be!

And the sun went down, and the crimson flush in the sky and on the sea faded out, the sea grew grey and crested with the white billows, which came racing in and broke upon the shore, roaring sullenly and raking back the pebbles with a sharp rattle at each recoil. The siren could sing no longer; her voice died away, and she gazed on the troubled sea with a wistful sadness in her great eyes.

At last a wave larger than the others struck the face of the low cliff with a shock that seemed to leave it trembling, and sent the cold salt spray dashing up into the siren's face.

She sprang forward to the edge and looked over, with a sudden terror lest the ledge below should be bare—but her victim lay there still, bound fast by her spell, and careless of the death that was advancing upon him.

Then she knew for the first time that she could not give him up to the sea, and she leaned down to him and laid one small white hand upon his shoulder. 'The next wave will carry you away,' she cried, trembling; 'there is still time; save yourself, for I cannot let you die!'

But he gave no sign of having heard her, but lay there motionless, and the wind wailed past them and the sea grew wilder and louder.

She remembered now that no efforts of his own could save him—he was doomed, and she was the cause of it, and she hid her face in her slender hands, weeping for the first time in her life.

The words he had spoken in answer to her questions about love came back to her: 'It was true, then,' she said to herself; 'it is love that I feel for him. But I cannot love—I must not love him—for if I do, my power is gone, and I must throw myself into the sea!'

So she hardened her heart once more, and turned away, for she feared to die; but again the ground shook beneath her, and the spray rose high into the air, and then she could bear it no more—whatever it cost her, she must save him—for if he died, what good would her life be to her?

'If one of us must die,' she said, 'I will be that one. I am cruel and wicked, as he told me; I have done harm enough!' and bending down, she wound her arms round his unconscious body and drew him gently up to the level above.

'You are safe now,' she whispered; 'you shall not be drowned—for I love you. Sail back to your maiden on the mainland, and be happy; but do not hate me for the evil I have wrought, for suffering and death have come to me in my turn!'

The lethargy into which he had fallen left him under her clinging embrace, and the sad, tender words fell almost unconsciously upon his dulled ears; he felt the touch of her hair as it brushed his cheek, and his forehead was still warm with the kiss she had pressed there as he opened his eyes—only to find himself alone.

For the fate which the siren had dreaded had come upon her at last; she had loved, and she had paid the penalty for loving, and never more would her wild, sweet voice beguile mortals to their doom.

## THE CURSE OF THE CATAFALQUES

I

Unless I am very much mistaken, until the time when I was subjected to the strange and exceptional experience which I now propose to relate, I had never been brought into close contact with anything of a supernatural description. At least if I ever was, the circumstance can have made no lasting impression upon me, as I am quite unable to recall it. But in the 'Curse of the Catafalques' I was confronted with a horror so weird and so altogether unusual, that I doubt whether I shall ever succeed in wholly forgetting it—and I know that I have never felt really well since.

It is difficult for me to tell my story intelligibly without some account of my previous history by way of introduction, although I will to make it as little diffuse as I may.

I had not been a success at home; I was an orphan, and, in my anxiety to please a wealthy uncle upon whom I was practically dependent, I had consented to submit myself to a series of competitive examinations for quite a variety of professions, but in each successive instance I achieved the same disheartening failure. Some explanation of this may, no doubt, be found in the fact that, with a fatal want of forethought, I had entirely omitted to prepare myself by any particular course of study—which, as I discovered too late, is almost indispensable to success in these intellectual contests.

My uncle himself took this view, and conceiving—not without discernment—that I was by no means likely to retrieve myself by any severe degree of application in the future, he had me shipped out to Australia, where he had correspondents and friends who would put things in my way.

They did put several things in my way—and, as might have been expected, I came to grief over every one of them, until at length, having given a fair trial to each opening that had been provided for me, I began to perceive that my uncle had made a grave mistake in believing me suited for a colonial career.

I resolved to return home and convince him of his error, and give him one more opportunity of repairing it; he had failed to discover the best means of utilising my undoubted ability, yet I would not reproach him (nor do I reproach him even now), for I too have felt the difficulty.

In pursuance of my resolution, I booked my passage home by one of the Orient liners from Melbourne to London. About an hour before the ship was to leave her moorings, I went on board and made my way at once to the state-room which I was to share with a fellow passenger, whose acquaintance I then made for the first time.

He was a tall cadaverous young man of about my own age, and my first view of him was not encouraging, for when I came in, I found him rolling restlessly on the cabin floor, and uttering hollow groans.

'This will never do,' I said, after I had introduced myself; 'if you're like this now, my good sir, what will you be when we're fairly out at sea? You must husband your resources for that. And why trouble to roll? The ship will do all that for you, if you will only have patience.'

He explained, somewhat brusquely, that he was suffering from mental agony, not sea-sickness; and by a little pertinacious questioning (for I would not allow myself to be rebuffed) I was soon in possession of the secret which was troubling my companion, whose name, as I also learned, was Augustus McFadden.

It seemed that his parents had emigrated before his birth, and he had lived all his life in the Colony, where he was contented and fairly prosperous—when an eccentric old aunt of his over in England happened to die.

She left McFadden himself nothing, having given by her will the bulk of her property to the only daughter of a baronet of ancient family, in whom she took a strong interest. But the will was not without its effect upon her existence, for it expressly mentioned the desire of the testatrix that the baronet should receive her nephew Augustus if he presented himself within a certain time, and should afford him every facility for proving his fitness for acceptance as a suitor. The alliance was merely recommended, however, not enjoined, and the gift was unfettered by any conditions.

'I heard of it first,' said McFadden, 'from Chlorine's father (Chlorine is her name, you know). Sir Paul Catafalque wrote to me, informing me of the mention of my name in my aunt's will, enclosing his daughter's photograph, and formally inviting me to come over and do my best, if my affections were not pre-engaged, to carry out the last wishes of the departed. He added that I might expect to receive shortly a packet from my aunt's executors which would explain matters fully, and in which I should find certain directions for my guidance. The photograph decided me; it was so eminently pleasing that I felt at once that my poor aunt's wishes must be sacred to me. I could not wait for the packet to arrive, and so I wrote at once to Sir Paul accepting the invitation. Yes,' he added, with another of the hollow groans, 'miserable wretch that I am, I pledged my honour to present myself as a suitor, and now—now—here I am, actually embarked upon the desperate errand!'

He seemed inclined to begin to roll again here, but I stopped him. 'Really,' I said, 'I think in your place, with an excellent chance—for I presume the lady's heart is also disengaged—with an excellent chance of winning a baronet's daughter with a considerable fortune and a pleasing appearance, I should bear up better.'

'You think so,' he rejoined, 'but you do not know all! The very day after I had despatched my fatal letter, my aunt's explanatory packet arrived. I tell you that when I read the hideous revelations it contained, and knew to what horrors I had innocently pledged myself, my hair stood on end, and I believe it has remained on end ever since. But it was too late. Here I am, engaged to carry out a task from which my inmost soul recoils. Ah, if I dared but retract!'

'Then why in the name of common sense, don't you retract?' I asked. 'Write and say that you much regret that a previous engagement, which you had unfortunately overlooked, deprives you of the pleasure of accepting.'

'Impossible,' he said; 'it would be agony to me to feel that I had incurred Chlorine's contempt, even though I only know her through a photograph at present. If I were to back out of it now, she would have reason to despise me, would she not?'

'Perhaps she would,' I said.

'You see my dilemma—I cannot retract; on the other hand, I dare not go on. The only thing, as I have thought lately, which could save me and my honour at the same time would be my death on the voyage out, for then my cowardice would remain undiscovered.'

'Well,' I said, 'you can die on the voyage out if you want to—there need be no difficulty about that. All you have to do is just to slip over the side some dark night when no one is looking. I tell you what,' I added (for somehow I began to feel a friendly interest in this poor slack-baked creature): 'if you don't find your nerves equal to it when it comes to the point, I don't mind giving you a leg over myself.'

'I never intended to go as far as that,' he said, rather pettishly, and without any sign of gratitude for my offer; 'I don't care about actually dying, if she could only be made to believe I had died that would be quite enough for me. I could live on here, happy in the thought that I was saved from her scorn. But how can she be made to believe it?—that's the point.'

'Precisely,' I said. 'You can hardly write yourself and inform her that you died on the voyage. You might do this, though: sail to England as you propose, and go to see her under another name, and break the sad intelligence to her.'

'Why, to be sure, I might do that!' he said, with some animation; 'I should certainly not be recognised— she can have no photograph of me, for I have never been photographed. And yet—no,' he added, with a shudder, 'it is useless. I can't do it; I dare not trust myself under that roof! I must find some other way. You have given me an idea. Listen,' he said, after a short pause: 'you seem to take an interest in me; you are going to London; the Catafalques live there, or near it, at some place called Parson's Green. Can I ask a great favour of you—would you very much mind seeking them out yourself as a fellow-voyager of mine? I could not expect you to tell a positive untruth on my account—but if, in the course of an interview with Chlorine, you could contrive to convey the impression that I died on my way to her side, you would be doing me a service I can never repay!'

'I should very much prefer to do you a service that you could repay,' was my very natural rejoinder.

'She will not require strict proof,' he continued eagerly; 'I could give you enough papers and things to convince her that you come from me. Say you will do me this kindness!'

I hesitated for some time longer, not so much, perhaps, from scruples of a conscientious kind as from a disinclination to undertake a troublesome commission for an entire stranger—gratuitously. But McFadden pressed me hard, and at length he made an appeal to springs in my nature which are never touched in vain, and I yielded.

When we had settled the question in its financial aspect, I said to McFadden, 'The only thing now is— how would you prefer to pass away? Shall I make you fall over and be devoured by a shark? That would be a picturesque end—and I could do myself justice over the shark? I should make the young lady weep considerably.'

'That won't do at all!' he said irritably; 'I can see from her face that Chlorine is a girl of a delicate sensibility, and would be disgusted by the idea of any suitor of hers spending his last cohesive moments inside such a beastly repulsive thing as a shark. I don't want to be associated in her mind with anything so unpleasant. No, sir; I will die—if you will oblige me by remembering it—of a low fever, of a non-infectious type, at sunset, gazing at her portrait with my fading eyesight and gasping her name with my last breath. She will cry more over that!'

'I might work it up into something effective, certainly,' I admitted; 'and, by the way, if you are going to expire in my state-room, I ought to know a little more about you than I do. There is time still before the tender goes; you might do worse than spend it in coaching me in your life's history.'

He gave me a few leading facts, and supplied me with several documents for study on the voyage; he even abandoned to me the whole of his travelling arrangements, which proved far more complete and serviceable than my own.

And then the 'All-ashore' bell rang, and McFadden, as he bade me farewell, took from his pocket a bulky packet. 'You have saved me,' he said. 'Now I can banish every recollection of this miserable episode. I need no longer preserve my poor aunt's directions; let them go, then.'

Before I could say anything, he had fastened something heavy to the parcel and dropped it through the cabin-light into the sea, after which he went ashore, and I have never seen nor heard of him since.

During the voyage I had leisure to think seriously over the affair, and the more I thought of the task I had undertaken, the less I liked it.

No man with the instincts of a gentleman can feel any satisfaction at rinding himself on the way to harrow up a poor young lady's feelings by a perfectly fictitious account of the death of a poor-spirited suitor who could selfishly save his reputation at her expense.

And so strong was my feeling about this from the very first, that I doubt whether, if McFadden's terms had been a shade less liberal, I could ever have brought myself to consent.

But it struck me that, under judiciously sympathetic treatment, the lady might prove not inconsolable, and that I myself might be able to heal the wound I was about to inflict.

I found a subtle pleasure in the thought of this, for, unless McFadden had misinformed me, Chlorine's fortune was considerable, and did not depend upon any marriage she might or might not make. On the other hand, I was penniless, and it seemed to me only too likely that her parents might seek to found some objection to me on that ground.

I studied the photograph McFadden had left with me; it was that of a pensive but distinctly pretty face, with an absence of firmness in it that betrayed a plastic nature. I felt certain that if I only had the recommendation, as McFadden had, of an aunt's dying wishes, it would not take me long to effect a complete conquest.

And then, as naturally as possible, came the thought—why should not I procure myself the advantages of this recommendation? Nothing could be easier; I had merely to present myself as Augustus McFadden, who was hitherto a mere name to them; the information I already possessed as to his past life would enable me to support the character, and as it seemed that the baronet lived in great seclusion, I could easily contrive to keep out of the way of the few friends and relations I had in London until my position was secure.

What harm would this innocent deception do to anyone? McFadden, even if he ever knew, would have no right to complain—he had given up all pretentions himself and if he was merely anxious to preserve his reputation, his wishes would be more than carried out, for I flattered myself that whatever ideal Chlorine might have formed of her destined suitor, I should come much nearer to it than poor McFadden could ever have done. No, he would gain, positively gain, by my assumption. He could not have counted upon arousing more than a mild regret as it was; now he would be fondly, it might be madly, loved. By proxy, it is true, but that was far more than he deserved.

Chlorine was not injured—far from it; she would have a suitor to welcome, not weep over, and his mere surname could make no possible difference to her. And lastly, it was a distinct benefit to me, for with a new name and an excellent reputation success would be an absolute certainty. What wonder, then, that the scheme, which opened out a far more manly and honourable means of obtaining a livelihood than any I had previously contemplated, should have grown more attractively feasible each day, until I resolved at last to carry it out? Let rigid moralists blame me if they will; I have never pretended to be better than the average run of mankind (though I am certainly no worse), and no one who really knows what human nature is will reproach me very keenly for obeying what was almost an instinct. And I may say this, that if ever an unfortunate man was bitterly punished for a fraud which was harmless, if not actually pious, by a visitation of intense and protracted terror, that person was I!

II

After arriving in England, and before presenting myself at Parson's Green in my assumed character, I took one precaution against any danger there might be of my throwing away my liberty in a fit of youthful impulsiveness. I went to Somerset House, and carefully examined the probate copy of the late Miss Petronia McFadden's last will and testament.

Nothing could have been more satisfactory; a sum of between forty and fifty thousand pounds was Chlorine's unconditionally, just as McFadden had said. I searched, but could find nothing in the will whatever to prevent her property, under the then existing state of the law, from passing under the entire control of a future husband.

After this, then, I could no longer restrain my ardour, and so, one foggy afternoon about the middle of December, I found myself driving towards the house in which I reckoned upon achieving a comfortable independence.

Parson's Green was reached at last; a small triangular open space bordered on two of its sides by mean and modern erections, but on the third by some ancient mansions, gloomy and neglected-looking indeed, but with traces on them still of their former consequence.

My cab stopped before the gloomiest of them all—a square grim house with dull and small-paned windows, flanked by two narrow and projecting wings, and built of dingy brick, faced with yellow-stone. Some old scroll-work railings, with a corroded frame in the middle for a long departed oil-lamp, separated the house from the road; inside was a semicircular patch of rank grass, and a damp gravel sweep led from the heavy gate to a square portico supported by two wasted black wooden pillars.

As I stood there, after pulling the pear-shaped bell-handle, and heard the bell tinkling and jangling fretfully within, and as I glanced up at the dull house-front looming cheerless out of the fog-laden December twilight, I felt my confidence beginning to abandon me for the first time, and I really was almost inclined to give the whole thing up and run away.

Before I could make up my mind, a mouldy and melancholy butler had come slowly down the sweep and opened the gate—and my opportunity had fled. Later I remembered how, as I walked along the gravel, a wild and wailing scream pierced the heavy silence—it seemed at once a lamentation and a warning. But as the District Railway was quite near, I did not attach any particular importance to the sound at the time.

I followed the butler through a dank and chilly hall, where an antique lamp hung glimmering feebly through its panes of dusty stained glass, up a broad carved staircase, and along some tortuous panelled passages, until at length I was ushered into a long and rather low reception room, scantily furnished with the tarnished mirrors and spindle-legged brocaded furniture of a bygone century.

A tall and meagre old man, with a long white beard, and haggard, sunken black eyes, was seated at one side of the high chimney-piece, while opposite him sat a little limp old lady with a nervous expression, and dressed in trailing black robes relieved by a little yellow lace about the head and throat. As I saw them, I recognised at once that I was in the presence of Sir Paul Catafalque and his wife.

They both rose slowly, and advanced arm-in-arm in their old-fashioned way, and met me with a stately solemnity. 'You are indeed welcome,' they said in faint hollow voices. 'We thank you for this proof of your chivalry and devotion. It cannot be but that such courage and such self-sacrifice will meet with their reward!'

And although I did not quite understand how they could have discerned, as yet, that I was chivalrous and devoted, I was too glad to have made a good impression to do anything but beg them not to mention it.

And then a slender figure, with a drooping head, a wan face, and large sad eyes, came softly down the dimly-lighted room towards me, and I and my destined bride met for the first time.

As I had expected, after she had once anxiously raised her eyes, and allowed them to rest upon me, her face was lighted up by an evident relief, as she discovered that the fulfilment of my aunt's wishes would not be so distasteful to her, personally, as it might have been.

For myself, I was upon the whole rather disappointed in her; the portrait had flattered her considerably—the real Chlorine was thinner and paler than I had been led to anticipate, while there was a settled melancholy in her manner which I felt would prevent her from being an exhilarating companion.

And I must say I prefer a touch of archness and animation in womankind, and, if I had been free to consult my own tastes, should have greatly preferred to become a member of a more cheerful family. Under the circumstances, however, I was not entitled to be too particular, and I put up with it.

From the moment of my arrival I fell easily and naturally into the position of an honoured guest, who might be expected in time to form nearer and dearer relations with the family, and certainly I was afforded every opportunity of doing so.

I made no mistakes, for the diligence with which I had got up McFadden's antecedents enabled me to give perfectly satisfactory replies to most of the few allusions or questions that were addressed to me, and I drew upon my imagination for the rest.

But those days I spent in the baronet's family were far from lively: the Catafalques went nowhere; they seemed to know nobody; at least no visitors ever called or dined there while I was with them, and the time dragged slowly on in a terrible monotony in that dim tomb of a house, which I was not expected to leave except for very brief periods, for Sir Paul would grow uneasy if I walked out alone—even to Putney.

There was something, indeed, about the attitude of both the old people towards myself which I could only consider as extremely puzzling. They would follow me about with a jealous care, blended with anxious alarm, and their faces as they looked at me wore an expression of tearful admiration, touched with something of pity, as for some youthful martyr; at times, too, they spoke of the gratitude they felt, and professed a determined hopefulness as to my ultimate success.

Now I was well aware that this is not the ordinary bearing of the parents of an heiress to a suitor who, however deserving in other respects, is both obscure and penniless, and the only way in which I could account for it was by the supposition that there was some latent defect in Chlorine's temper or constitution, which entitled the man who won her to commiseration, and which would also explain their evident anxiety to get her off their hands.

But although anything of this kind would be, of course, a drawback, I felt that forty or fifty thousand pounds would be a fair set-off—and I could not expect everything.

When the time came at which I felt that I could safely speak to Chlorine of what lay nearest my heart, I found an unforeseen difficulty in bringing her to confess that she reciprocated my passion.

She seemed to shrink unaccountably from speaking the word which gave me the right to claim her, confessing that she dreaded it not for her own sake, but for mine alone, which struck me as an unpleasantly morbid trait in so young a girl.

Again and again I protested that I was willing to run all risks—as I was—and again and again she resisted, though always more faintly, until at last my efforts were successful, and I forced from her lips the assent which was of so much importance to me.

But it cost her a great effort, and I believe she even swooned immediately afterwards; but this is only conjecture, as I lost no time in seeking Sir Paul and clenching the matter before Chlorine had time to retract.

He heard what I had to tell him with a strange light of triumph and relief in his weary eyes. 'You have made an old man very happy and hopeful,' he said. 'I ought, even now to deter you, but I am too selfish for that. And you are young and brave and ardent; why need we despair? I suppose,' he added, looking keenly at me, 'you would prefer as little delay as possible?'

'I should indeed,' I replied. I was pleased, for I had not expected to find him so sensible as that.

'Then leave all preliminaries to me; when the day and time have been settled, I will let you know. As you are aware, it will be necessary to have your signature to this document; and here, my boy, I must in conscience warn you solemnly that by signing you make your decision irrevocable—irrevocable, you understand?'

When I had heard this, I need scarcely say that I was all eagerness to sign; so great was my haste that I did not even try to decipher the somewhat crabbed and antiquated writing in which the terms of the agreement were set out.

I was anxious to impress the baronet with a sense of my gentlemanly feeling and the confidence I had in him, while I naturally presumed that, since the contract was binding upon me, the baronet would, as a man of honour, hold it equally conclusive on his own side.

As I look back upon it now, it seems simply extraordinary that I should have been so easily satisfied, have taken so little pains to find out the exact position in which I was placing myself; but, with the ingenuous confidence of youth, I fell an easy victim, as I was to realise later with terrible enlightenment.

'Say nothing of this to Chlorine,' said Sir Paul, as I handed him the document signed, 'until the final arrangements are made; it will only distress her unnecessarily.'

I wondered why at the time, but I promised to obey, supposing that he knew best, and for some days after that I made no mention to Chlorine of the approaching day which was to witness our union.

As we were continually together, I began to regard her with an esteem which I had not thought possible at first. Her looks improved considerably under the influence of happiness, and I found she could converse intelligently enough upon several topics, and did not bore me nearly as much as I was fully prepared for.

And so the time passed less heavily, until one afternoon the baronet took me aside mysteriously. 'Prepare yourself, Augustus' (they had all learned to call me Augustus), he said; 'all is arranged. The event upon which our dearest hopes depend is fixed for to-morrow—in the Grey Chamber of course, and at midnight.'

I thought this a curious time and place for the ceremony, but I had divined his eccentric passion for privacy and retirement, and only imagined that he had procured some very special form of licence.

'But you do not know the Grey Chamber,' he added. 'Come with me, and I will show you where it is.' And he led me up the broad staircase, and, stopping at the end of a passage before an immense door covered with black baize and studded with brass nails, which gave it a hideous resemblance to a gigantic coffin lid, he pressed a spring, and it fell slowly back.

I saw a long dim gallery, whose very existence nothing in the external appearance of the mansion had led me to suspect; it led to a heavy oaken door with cumbrous plates and fastenings of metal.

'To-morrow night is Christmas Eve, as you are doubtless aware,' he said in a hushed voice. 'At twelve, then, you will present yourself at yonder door—the door of the Grey Chamber—where you must fulfil the engagement you have made.'

I was surprised at his choosing such a place for the ceremony; it would have been more cheerful in the long drawing room; but it was evidently a whim of his, and I was too happy to think of opposing it. I hastened at once to Chlorine, with her father's sanction, and told her that the crowning moment of both our lives was fixed at last.

The effect of my announcement was astonishing: she fainted, for which I remonstrated with her as soon as she came to herself. 'Such extreme sensitiveness, my love,' I could not help saying, 'may be highly creditable to your sense of maidenly propriety, but allow me to say that I can scarcely regard it as a compliment.'

'Augustus,' she said, 'you must not think I doubt you; and yet—and yet—the ordeal will be a severe one for you.'

'I will steel my nerves,' I said grimly (for I was annoyed with her); 'and, after all, Chlorine, the ceremony is not invariably fatal; I have heard of the victim surviving it—occasionally.'

'How brave you are!' she said earnestly. 'I will imitate you, Augustus; I too will hope.'

I really thought her insane, which alarmed me for the validity of the marriage. 'Yes, I am weak, foolish, I know,' she continued; 'but oh, I shudder so when I think of you, away in that gloomy Grey Chamber, going through it all alone!'

This confirmed my worst fears. No wonder her parents felt grateful to me for relieving them of such a responsibility! 'May I ask where you intend to be at the time?' I inquired very quietly.

'You will not think us unfeeling,' she replied, 'but dear papa considered that such anxiety as ours would be scarcely endurable did we not seek some distraction from it; and so, as a special favour, he has procured evening orders for Sir John Soane's Museum in Lincoln's Inn Fields, where we shall drive immediately after dinner.'

I knew that the proper way to treat the insane was by reasoning with them gently, so as to place their own absurdity clearly before them. 'If you are forgetting your anxiety in Sir John Soane's Museum, while I cool my heels in the Grey Chamber,' I said, 'is it probable that any clergyman will be induced to perform the marriage ceremony? Did you really think two people can be united separately?'

She was astonished this time. 'You are joking!' she cried; 'you cannot really believe that we are to be married in—in the Grey Chamber?'

'Then will you tell me where we are to be married?' I asked. 'I think I have the right to know—it can hardly be at the Museum!'

She turned upon me with a sudden misgiving; 'I could almost fancy,' she said anxiously, 'that this is no feigned ignorance. Augustus, your aunt sent you a message—tell me, have you read it?'

Now, owing to McFadden's want of consideration, this was my one weak point—I had not read it, and thus I felt myself upon delicate ground. The message evidently related to business of importance which was to be transacted in this Grey Chamber, and as the genuine McFadden clearly knew all about it, it would have been simply suicidal to confess my own ignorance.

'Why of course, darling, of course,' I said hastily. 'You must think no more of my silly joke; there is something I have to arrange in the Grey Chamber before I can call you mine. But, tell me, why does it make you so uneasy?' I added, thinking it might be prudent to find out beforehand what formality was expected from me.

'I cannot help it—no, I cannot!' she cried, 'the test is so searching—are you sure that you are prepared at all points? I overheard my father say that no precaution could safely be neglected. I have such a terrible foreboding that, after all, this may come between us.'

It was clear enough to me now; the baronet was by no means so simple and confiding in his choice of a son-in-law as I had imagined, and had no intention, after all, of accepting me without some inquiry into my past life, my habits, and my prospects.

That he should seek to make this examination more impressive by appointing this ridiculous midnight interview for it, was only what might have been expected from an old man of his confirmed eccentricity.

But I knew I could easily contrive to satisfy the baronet, and with the idea of consoling Chlorine, I said as much. 'Why will you persist in treating me like a child, Augustus?' she broke out almost petulantly. 'They have tried to hide it all from me, but do you suppose I do not know that in the Grey Chamber you will have to encounter one far more formidable, far more difficult to satisfy, than poor dear papa?'

'I see you know more than I—more than I thought you did,' I said. 'Let us understand one another, Chlorine—tell me exactly how much you know.'

'I have told you all I know,' she said; 'it is your turn to confide in me.'

'Not even for your sweet sake, my dearest,' I was obliged to say, 'can I break the seal that is set upon my tongue. You must not press me. Come, let us talk of other things.'

But I now saw that matters were worse than I had thought; instead of the feeble old baronet I should have to deal with a stranger, some exacting and officious friend or relation perhaps, or, more probably, a keen family solicitor who would put questions I should not care about answering, and even be capable of insisting upon strict settlements.

It was that, of course; they would try to tie my hands by a strict settlement, with a brace of cautious trustees; unless I was very careful, all I should get by my marriage would be a paltry life-interest, contingent upon my surviving my wife.

This revolted me; it seems to me that when law comes in with its offensively suspicious restraints upon the husband and its indelicately premature provisions for the offspring, all the poetry of love is gone at once. By allowing the wife to receive the income 'for her separate use and free from the control of her husband,' as the phrase runs, you infallibly brush the bloom from the peach, and implant the 'little speck within the fruit' which, as Tennyson beautifully says, will widen by-and-by and make the music mute.

This may be overstrained on my part, but it represents my honest conviction; I was determined to have nothing to do with law. If it was necessary, I felt quite sure enough of Chlorine to defy Sir Paul. I would refuse to meet a family solicitor anywhere, and I intended to say so plainly at the first convenient opportunity.


III

The opportunity came after dinner that evening when we were all in the drawing-room, Lady Catafalque dozing uneasily in her arm-chair behind a firescreen, and Chlorine, in the further room, playing funereal dirges in the darkness, and pressing the stiff keys of the old piano with a languid uncertain touch.

Drawing a chair up to Sir Paul's, I began to broach the subject calmly and temperately. 'I find,' I said, 'that we have not quite understood one another over this affair in the Grey Chamber. When I agreed to an appointment there, I thought—well, it doesn't matter what I thought, I was a little too premature. What I want to say now is, that while I have no objection to you, as Chlorine's father, asking me any questions (in reason) about myself, I feel a delicacy in discussing my private affairs with a perfect stranger.'

His burning eyes looked me through and through; 'I don't understand,' he said. 'Tell me what you are talking about.'

I began all over again, telling him exactly what I felt about solicitors and settlements. 'Are you well?' he asked sternly. 'What have I ever said about settlements or solicitors?

I saw that I was wrong again, and could only stammer something to the effect that a remark of Chlorine's had given me this impression.

'What she could have said to convey such an idea passes my comprehension,' he said gravely; 'but she knows nothing—she's a mere child. I have felt from the first, my boy, that your aunt's intention was to benefit you quite as much as my own daughter. Believe me, I shall not attempt to restrict you in any way; I shall be too rejoiced to see you come forth in safety from the Grey Chamber.'

All the relief I had begun to feel respecting the settlements was poisoned by these last words. Why did he talk of that confounded Grey Chamber as if it were a fiery furnace, or a cage of lions? What mystery was there concealed beneath all this, and how, since I was obviously supposed to be thoroughly acquainted with it, could I manage to penetrate the secret of this perplexing appointment?

While he had been speaking, the faint, mournful music died away, and, looking up, I saw Chlorine, a pale, slight form, standing framed in the archway which connected the two rooms.

'Go back to your piano, my child,' said the baronet; 'Augustus and I have much to talk about which is not for your ears.'

'But why not?' she said; 'oh, why not? Papa! dearest mother! Augustus! I can bear it no longer! I have often felt of late that we are living this strange life under the shadow of some fearful Thing, which would chase all cheerfulness from any home. More than this I did not seek to know; I dared not ask. But now, when I know that Augustus, whom I love with my whole heart, must shortly face this ghastly presence, you cannot wonder if I seek to learn the real extent of the danger that awaits him! Tell me all. I can bear the worst—for it cannot be more horrible than my own fears!'

Lady Catafalque had roused herself and was wringing her long mittened hands and moaning feebly. 'Paul,' she said, 'you must not tell her; it will kill her; she is not strong!' Her husband seemed undecided, and I myself began to feel exquisitely uncomfortable. Chlorine's words pointed to something infinitely more terrible than a mere solicitor.

'Poor girl,' said Sir Paul at last, 'it was for your own good that the whole truth has been thus concealed from you; but now, perhaps, the time has come when the truest kindness will be to reveal all. What do you say, Augustus?'

'I—I agree with you,' I replied faintly; 'she ought to be told.'

'Precisely!' he said. 'Break to her, then, the nature of the ordeal which lies before you.'

It was the very thing which I wanted to be broken to me! I would have given the world to know all about it myself, and so I stared at his gloomy old face with eyes that must have betrayed my helpless dismay. At last I saved myself by suggesting that such a story would come less harshly from a parent's lips.

'Well, so be it,' he said. 'Chlorine, compose yourself, dearest one; sit down there, and summon up all your fortitude to hear what I am about to tell you. You must know, then—I think you had better let your mother give you a cup of tea before I begin; it will steady your nerves.'

During the delay which followed—for Sir Paul did not consider his daughter sufficiently fortified until she had taken at least three cups—I suffered tortures of suspense, which I dared not betray.

They never thought of offering me any tea, though the merest observer might have noticed how very badly I wanted it.

At last the baronet was satisfied, and not without a sort of gloomy enjoyment and a proud relish of the distinction implied in his exceptional affliction, he began his weird and almost incredible tale.

'It is now,' said he, 'some centuries since our ill-fated house was first afflicted with the family curse which still attends it. A certain Humfrey de Catafalque, by his acquaintance with the black art, as it was said, had procured the services of a species of familiar, a dread and supernatural being. For some reason he had conceived a bitter enmity towards his nearest relations, whom he hated with a virulence that not even death could soften. For, by a refinement of malice, he bequeathed this baleful thing to his descendants for ever, as an inalienable heirloom! And to this day it follows the title—and the head of the family for the time being is bound to provide it with a secret apartment under his own roof. But that is not the worst: as each member of our house succeeds to the ancestral rank and honours, he must seek an interview with 'The Curse,' as it has been styled for generations. And, in that interview, it is decided whether the spell is to be broken and the Curse depart from us for ever—or whether it is to continue its blighting influence, and hold yet another life in miserable thraldom.'

'And are you one of its thralls then, papa?' faltered Chlorine.

'I am, indeed,' he said. 'I failed to quell it, as every Catafalque, however brave and resolute, has failed yet. It checks all my accounts, and woe to me if that cold, withering eye discovers the slightest error—even in the pence column! I could not describe the extent of my bondage to you, my daughter, or the humiliation of having to go and tremble monthly before that awful presence. Not even yet, old as I am, have I grown quite accustomed to it!'

Never, in my wildest imaginings, had I anticipated anything one quarter so dreadful as this; but still I clung to the hope that it was impossible to bring me into the affair.

'But, Sir Paul,' I said—'Sir Paul, you—you mustn't stop there, or you'll alarm Chlorine more than there's any need to do. She—ha, ha!—don't you see, she has got some idea into her head that I have to go through much the same sort of thing. Just explain that to her. I'm not a Catafalque, Chlorine, so it—it can't interfere with me. That is so, isn't it, Sir Paul? Good heavens, sir, don't torture her like this!' I cried, as he was silent. 'Speak out!'

'You mean well, Augustus,' he said, 'but the time for deceiving her has gone by; she must know the worst. Yes, my poor child,' he continued to Chlorine, whose eyes were wide with terror—though I fancy mine were even wider—'unhappily, though our beloved Augustus is not a Catafalque himself, he has of his own free will brought himself within the influence of the Curse, and he, too, at the appointed hour, must keep the awful assignation, and brave all that the most fiendish malevolence can do to shake his resolution.'

I could not say a single word; the horror of the idea was altogether too much for me, and I fell back on my chair in a state of speechless collapse.

'You see,' Sir Paul went on explaining, 'it is not only all new baronets, but every one who would seek an alliance with the females of our race, who must, by the terms of that strange bequest, also undergo this trial. It may be in some degree owing to this necessity that, ever since Humfrey de Catafalque's diabolical testament first took effect, every maiden of our House has died a spinster.' (Here Chlorine hid her face with a low wail.) 'In 1770, it is true, one solitary suitor was emboldened by love and daring to face the ordeal. He went calmly and resolutely to the chamber where the Curse was then lodged, and the next morning they found him outside the door—a gibbering maniac!'

I writhed on my chair. 'Augustus!' cried Chlorine wildly, 'promise me you will not permit the Curse to turn you into a gibbering maniac. I think if I saw you gibber I should die!'

I was on the verge of gibbering then; I dared not trust myself to speak.

'Nay, Chlorine,' said Sir Paul more cheerfully, 'there is no cause for alarm; all has been made smooth for Augustus.' (I began to brighten a little at this.) 'His Aunt Petronia had made a special study of the old-world science of incantation, and had undoubtedly succeeded at last in discovering the master-word which, employed according to her directions, would almost certainly break the unhallowed spell. In her compassionate attachment to us, she formed the design of persuading a youth of blameless life and antecedents to present himself as our champion, and the reports she had been given of our dear Augustus' irreproachable character led her to select him as a likely instrument. And her confidence in his generosity and courage was indeed well-founded, for he responded at once to the appeal of his departed aunt, and, with her instructions for his safeguard, and the consciousness of his virtue as an additional protection, there is hope, my child, strong hope, that, though the struggle may be a long and bitter one, yet Augustus will emerge a victor!'

I saw very little ground for expecting to emerge as anything of the kind, or for that matter to emerge at all, except in instalments,—for the master-word which was to abash the demon was probably inside the packet of instructions, and that was certainly somewhere at the bottom of the sea, outside Melbourne, fathoms below the surface.

I could bear no more. 'It's simply astonishing to me,' I said, 'that in the nineteenth century, hardly six miles from Charing Cross, you can calmly allow this hideous "Curse," or whatever you call it, to have things all its own way like this.'

'What can I do, Augustus?' he asked helplessly.

'Do? Anything!' I retorted wildly (for I scarcely knew what I said). 'Take it out for an airing (it must want an airing by this time); take it out—and lose it! Or get both the archbishops to step in and lay it for you. Sell the house, and make the purchaser take it at a valuation, with the other fixtures. I certainly would not live under the same roof with it. And I want you to understand one thing—I was never told all this; I have been kept in the dark about it. Of course I knew there was some kind of a curse in the family—but I never dreamed of anything so bad as this, and I never had any intention of being boxed up alone with it either. I shall not go near the Grey Chamber!'

'Not go near it!' they all cried aghast.

'Not on any account,' I said, for I felt firmer and easier now that I had taken up this position. 'If the Curse has any business with me, let it come down and settle it here before you all in a plain straightforward manner. Let us go about it in a business-like way. On second thoughts,' I added, fearing lest they should find means of carrying out this suggestion. 'I won't meet it anywhere!'

'And why—why won't you meet it?' they asked breathlessly.

'Because,' I explained desperately, 'because I'm—I'm a materialist.' (I had not been previously aware that I had any decided opinions on the question, but I could not stay then to consider the point.) 'How can I have any dealings with a preposterous supernatural something which my reason forbids me to believe in? You see my difficulty? It would be inconsistent, to begin with, and—and extremely painful to both sides.'

'No more of this ribaldry,' said Sir Paul sternly. 'It may be terribly remembered against you when the hour comes. Keep a guard over your tongue, for all our sakes, and more especially your own. Recollect that the Curse knows all that passes beneath this roof. And do not forget, too, that you are pledged— irrevocably pledged. You must confront the Curse!'

Only a short hour ago, and I had counted Chlorine's fortune and Chlorine as virtually mine; and now I saw my golden dreams roughly shattered for ever! And, oh, what a wrench it was to tear myself from them! what it cost me to speak the words that barred my Paradise to me for ever!

But if I wished to avoid confronting the Curse—and I did wish this very much—I had no other course. 'I had no right to pledge myself,' I said, with quivering lips, 'under all the circumstances.'

'Why not,' they demanded again; 'what circumstances?'

'Well, in the first place,' I assured them earnestly, 'I'm a base impostor. I am indeed. I'm not Augustus McFadden at all. My real name is of no consequence—but it's a prettier one than that. As for McFadden, he, I regret to say, is now no more.'

Why on earth I could not have told the plain truth here has always been a mystery to me. I suppose I had been lying so long that it was difficult to break myself of this occasionally inconvenient trick at so short a notice, but I certainly mixed things up to a hopeless extent.

'Yes,' I continued mournfully, 'McFadden is dead; I will tell you how he died if you would care to know. During his voyage here he fell overboard, and was almost instantly appropriated by a gigantic shark, when, as I happened to be present, I enjoyed the melancholy privilege of seeing him pass away. For one brief moment I beheld him between the jaws of the creature, so pale but so composed (I refer to McFadden, you understand—not the shark), he threw just one glance up at me, and with a smile, the sad sweetness of which I shall never forget (it was McFadden's smile, I mean, of course—not the shark's), he, courteous and considerate to the last, requested me to break the news and remember him very kindly to you all. And, in the same instant, he abruptly vanished within the monster—and I saw neither of them again!'

Of course in bringing the shark in at all I was acting directly contrary to my instructions, but I quite forgot them in my anxiety to escape the acquaintance of the Curse of the Catafalques.

'If this is true, sir,' said the baronet haughtily when I had finished, 'you have indeed deceived us basely.'

'That,' I replied, 'is what I was endeavouring to bring out. You see, it puts it quite out of my power to meet your family Curse. I should not feel justified in intruding upon it. So, if you will kindly let some one fetch a fly or a cab in half an hour—'

'Stop!' cried Chlorine. 'Augustus, as I will call you still, you must not go like this. If you have stooped to deceit, it was for love of me, and—and Mr. McFadden is dead. If he had been alive, I should have felt it my duty to allow him an opportunity of winning my affection, but he is lying in his silent tomb, and—and I have learnt to love you. Stay, then; stay and brave the Curse; we may yet be happy!'

I saw how foolish I had been not to tell the truth at first, and I hastened to repair this error. 'When I described McFadden as dead,' I said hoarsely, 'it was a loose way of putting the facts—because, to be quite accurate, he isn't dead. We found out afterwards that it was another fellow the shark had swallowed, and, in fact, another shark altogether. So he is alive and well now, at Melbourne, but when he came to know about the Curse, he was too much frightened to come across, and he asked me to call and make his excuses. I have now done so, and will trespass no further on your kindness—if you will tell somebody to bring a vehicle of any sort in a quarter of an hour.'

'Pardon me,' said the baronet, 'but we cannot part in this way. I feared when first I saw you that your resolution might give way under the strain; it is only natural, I admit. But you deceive yourself if you think we cannot see that these extraordinary and utterly contradictory stories are prompted by sudden panic. I quite understand it, Augustus; I cannot blame you; but to allow you to withdraw now would be worse than weakness on my part. The panic will pass, you will forget these fears to-morrow, you must forget them; remember, you have promised. For your own sake, I shall take care that you do not forfeit that solemn bond, for I dare not let you run the danger of exciting the Curse by a deliberate insult.'

I saw clearly that his conduct was dictated by a deliberate and most repulsive selfishness; he did not entirely believe me, but he was determined that if there was any chance that I, whoever I might be, could free him from his present thraldom, he would not let it escape him.

I raved, I protested, I implored—all in vain; they would not believe a single word I said, they positively refused to release me, and insisted upon my performing my engagement.

And at last Chlorine and her mother left the room, with a little contempt for my unworthiness mingled with their evident compassion; and a little later Sir Paul conducted me to my room, and locked me in 'till,' as he said, 'I had returned to my senses.'


IV


What a night I passed, as I tossed sleeplessly from side to side under the canopy of my old-fashioned bedstead, torturing my fevered brain with vain speculations as to the fate the morrow was to bring me.

I felt myself perfectly helpless; I saw no way out of it; they seemed bent upon offering me up as a sacrifice to this private Moloch of theirs. The baronet was quite capable of keeping me locked up all the next day and pushing me into the Grey Chamber to take my chance when the hour came.

If I had only some idea what the Curse was like to look at, I thought I might not feel quite so afraid of it; the vague and impalpable awfulness of the thing was intolerable, and the very thought of it caused me to fling myself about in an ecstasy of horror.

By degrees, however, as daybreak came near, I grew calmer—until at length I arrived at a decision. It seemed evident to me that, as I could not avoid my fate, the wisest course was to go forth to meet it with as good a grace as possible. Then, should I by some fortunate accident come well out of it, my fortune was ensured.

But if I went on repudiating my assumed self to the very last, I should surely arouse a suspicion which the most signal rout of the Curse would not serve to dispel.

And after all, as I began to think, the whole thing had probably been much exaggerated; if I could only keep my head, and exercise all my powers of cool impudence, I might contrive to hoodwink this formidable relic of mediæval days, which must have fallen rather behind the age by this time. It might even turn out to be (although I was hardly sanguine as to this) as big a humbug as I was myself, and we should meet with confidential winks, like the two augurs.

But, at all events, I resolved to see this mysterious affair out, and trust to my customary good luck to bring me safely through, and so, having found the door unlocked, I came down to breakfast something like my usual self, and set myself to remove the unfavourable impression I had made on the previous night.

They did it from consideration for me, but still it was mistaken kindness for them all to leave me entirely to my own thoughts during the whole of the day, for I was driven to mope alone about the gloom-laden building, until by dinner-time I was very low indeed from nervous depression.

We dined in almost unbroken silence; now and then, as Sir Paul saw my hand approaching a decanter, he would open his lips to observe that I should need the clearest head and the firmest nerve ere long, and warn me solemnly against the brown sherry; from time to time, too, Chlorine and her mother stole apprehensive glances at me, and sighed heavily between every course. I never remember eating a dinner with so little enjoyment.

The meal came to an end at last; the ladies rose, and Sir Paul and I were left to brood over the dessert. I fancy both of us felt a delicacy in starting a conversation, and before I could hit upon a safe remark, Lady Catafalque and her daughter returned, dressed, to my unspeakable horror, in readiness to go out. Worse than that even, Sir Paul apparently intended to accompany them, for he rose at their entrance.

'It is now time for us to bid you a solemn farewell, Augustus,' he said, in his hollow old voice. 'You have three hours before you yet, and if you are wise, you will spend them in earnest self-preparation. At midnight, punctually, for you must not dare to delay, you will go to the Grey Chamber—the way thither you know, and you will find the Curse prepared for you. Good-bye, then, brave and devoted boy; stand firm, and no harm can befall you!'

'You are going away, all of you!' I cried. They were not what you might call a gay family to sit up with, but even their society was better than my own.

'Upon these dread occasions,' he explained, 'it is absolutely forbidden for any human being but one to remain in the house. All the servants have already left, and we are about to take our departure for a private hotel near the Strand. We shall just have time, if we start at once, to inspect the Soane Museum on our way thither, which will serve as some distraction from the terrible anxiety we shall be feeling.'

At this I believe I positively howled with terror; all my old panic came back with a rush. 'Don't leave me all alone with It!' I cried; 'I shall go mad if you do!'

Sir Paul simply turned on his heel in silent contempt, and his wife followed him; but Chlorine remained behind for one instant, and somehow, as she gazed at me with a yearning pity in her sad eyes, I thought I had never seen her looking so pretty before.

'Augustus,' she said, 'get up.' (I suppose I must have been on the floor somewhere.) 'Be a man; show us we were not mistaken in you. You know I would spare you this if I could; but we are powerless. Oh, be brave, or I shall lose you for ever!'

Her appeal did seem to put a little courage into me, I staggered up and kissed her slender hand and vowed sincerely to be worthy of her.

And then she too passed out, and the heavy hall door slammed behind the three, and the rusty old gate screeched like a banshee as it swung back and closed with a clang.

I heard the carriage-wheels grind the slush, and the next moment I knew that I was shut up on Christmas Eve in that sombre mansion—with the Curse of the Catafalques as my sole companion!

I don't think the generous ardour with which Chlorine's last words had inspired me lasted very long, for I caught myself shivering before the clock struck nine, and, drawing up a clumsy leathern arm-chair close to the fire, I piled on the logs and tried to get rid of a certain horrible sensation of internal vacancy which was beginning to afflict me.

I tried to look my situation fairly in the face; whatever reason and common sense had to say about it, there seemed no possible doubt that something of a supernatural order was shut up in that great chamber down the corridor, and also that, if I meant to win Chlorine, I must go up and have some kind of an interview with it. Once more I wished I had some definite idea to go upon; what description of being should I find this Curse? Would it be aggressively ugly, like the bogie of my infancy, or should I see a lank and unsubstantial shape, draped in clinging black, with nothing visible beneath it but a pair of burning hollow eyes and one long pale bony hand? Really I could not decide which would be the more trying of the two.

By-and-by I began to recollect unwillingly all the frightful stories I had ever read; one in particular came back to me,—the adventure of a foreign marshal who, after much industry, succeeded in invoking an evil spirit, which came bouncing into the room shaped like a gigantic ball, with, I think, a hideous face in the middle of it, and would not be got rid of until the horrified marshal had spent hours in hard praying and persistent exorcism!

What should I do if the Curse was a globular one and came rolling all round the room after me?

Then there was another appalling tale I had read in some magazine,—a tale of a secret chamber, too, and in some respects a very similar case to my own, for there the heir of some great house had to go in and meet a mysterious aged person with strange eyes and an evil smile, who kept attempting to shake hands with him.

Nothing should induce me to shake hands with the Curse of the Catafalques, however apparently friendly I might find it.

But it was not very likely to be friendly, for it was one of those mystic powers of darkness which know nearly everything—it would detect me as an impostor directly, and what would become of me? I declare I almost resolved to confess all and sob out my deceit upon its bosom, and the only thing which made me pause was the reflection that probably the Curse did not possess a bosom.

By this time I had worked myself up to such a pitch of terror that I found it absolutely necessary to brace my nerves, and I did brace them. I emptied all the three decanters, but as Sir Paul's cellar was none of the best, the only result was that, while my courage and daring were not perceptibly heightened, I was conscious of feeling exceedingly unwell.

Tobacco, no doubt, would have calmed and soothed me, but I did not dare to smoke. For the Curse, being old-fashioned, might object to the smell of it, and I was anxious to avoid exciting its prejudices unnecessarily.

And so I simply sat in my chair and shook. Every now and then I heard steps on the frosty path outside: sometimes a rapid tread, as of some happy person bound to scenes of Christmas revelry, and little dreaming of the miserable wretch he was passing; sometimes the slow creaking tramp of the Fulham policeman on his beat.

What if I called him in and gave the Curse into custody—either for putting me in bodily fear (as it was undeniably doing), or for being found on the premises under suspicious circumstances?

There was a certain audacity about this means of cutting the knot that fascinated me at first, but still I did not venture to adopt it, thinking it most probable that the stolid constable would decline to interfere as soon as he knew the facts; and even if he did, it would certainly annoy Sir Paul extremely to hear of his Family Curse spending its Christmas in a police-cell, and I felt instinctively that he would consider it a piece of unpardonable bad taste on my part.

So one hour passed. A few minutes after ten I heard more footsteps and voices in low consultation, as if a band of men had collected outside the railings. Could there be any indication without of the horrors these walls contained?

But no; the gaunt house-front kept its secret too well; they were merely the waits. They saluted me with the old carol, 'God rest you, merry gentleman, let nothing you dismay!' which should have encouraged me, but it didn't, and they followed that up by a wheezy but pathetic rendering of 'The Mistletoe Bough.'

For a time I did not object to them; while they were scraping and blowing outside I felt less abandoned and cut off from human help, and then they might arouse softer sentiments in the Curse upstairs by their seasonable strains: these things do happen at Christmas sometimes. But their performance was really so infernally bad that it was calculated rather to irritate than subdue any evil spirit, and very soon I rushed to the window and beckoned to them furiously to go away.

Unhappily, they thought I was inviting them indoors for refreshment, and came round to the gate, when they knocked and rang incessantly for a quarter of an hour.

This must have stirred the Curse up quite enough, but when they had gone, there came a man with a barrel organ, which was suffering from some complicated internal disorder, causing it to play its whole repertory at once, in maddening discords. Even the grinder himself seemed dimly aware that his instrument was not doing itself justice, for he would stop occasionally, as if to ponder or examine it. But he was evidently a sanguine person and had hopes of bringing it round by a little perseverance; so, as Parson's Green was well-suited by its quiet for this mode of treatment, he remained there till he must have reduced the Curse to a rampant and rabid condition.

He went at last, and then the silence that followed began to my excited fancy (for I certainly saw nothing) to be invaded by strange sounds that echoed about the old house. I heard sharp reports from the furniture, sighing moans in the draughty passages, doors opening and shutting, and—worse still—stealthy padding footsteps, both above and in the ghostly hall outside!

I sat there in an ice-cold perspiration, until my nerves required more bracing, to effect which I had recourse to the spirit-case.

And after a short time my fears began to melt away rapidly. What a ridiculous bugbear I was making of this thing after all! Was I not too hasty in setting it down as ugly and hostile before I had seen it ... how did I know it was anything which deserved my horror?

Here a gush of sentiment came over me at the thought that it might be that for long centuries the poor Curse had been cruelly misunderstood—that it might be a blessing in disguise.

I was so affected by the thought that I resolved to go up at once and wish it a merry Christmas through the keyhole, just to show that I came in no unfriendly spirit.

But would not that seem as if I was afraid of it? I scorned the idea of being afraid. Why, for two straws, I would go straight in and pull its nose for it—if it had a nose!

I went out with this object, not very steadily, but before I had reached the top of the dim and misty staircase, I had given up all ideas of defiance, and merely intended to go as far as the corridor by way of a preliminary canter.

The coffin-lid door stood open, and I looked apprehensively down the corridor; the grim metal fittings on the massive door of the Grey Chamber were gleaming with a mysterious pale light, something between the phenomena obtained by electricity and the peculiar phosphorescence observable in a decayed shell-fish; under the door I saw the reflection of a sullen red glow, and within I could hear sounds like the roar of a mighty wind, above which peals of fiendish mirth rang out at intervals, and were followed by a hideous dull clanking.

It seemed only too evident that the Curse was getting up the steam for our interview. I did not stay there long, because I was afraid that it might dart out suddenly and catch me eavesdropping, which would be a hopelessly bad beginning. I got back to the dining-room, somehow; the fire had taken advantage of my short absence to go out, and I was surprised to find by the light of the fast-dimming lamp that it was a quarter to twelve already.

Only fifteen more fleeting minutes and then—unless I gave up Chlorine and her fortune for ever—I must go up and knock at that awful door, and enter the presence of the frightful mystic Thing that was roaring and laughing and clanking on the other side!

Stupidly I sat and stared at the clock; in five minutes, now, I should be beginning my desperate duel with one of the powers of darkness—a thought which gave me sickening qualms.

I was clinging to the thought that I had still two precious minutes left—perhaps my last moments of safety and sanity—when the lamp expired with a gurgling sob, and left me in the dark.

I was afraid of sitting there all alone any longer, and besides, if I lingered, the Curse might come down and fetch me. The horror of this idea made me resolve to go up at once, especially as scrupulous punctuality might propitiate it.

Groping my way to the door, I reached the hall and stood there, swaying under the old stained-glass lantern. And then I made a terrible discovery. I was not in a condition to transact any business; I had disregarded Sir Paul's well-meant warning at dinner; I was not my own master. I was lost!

The clock in the adjoining room tolled twelve, and from without the distant steeples proclaimed in faint peals and chimes that it was Christmas morn. My hour had come!

Why did I not mount those stairs? I tried again and again, and fell down every time, and at each attempt I knew the Curse would be getting more and more impatient.

I was quite five minutes late, and yet, with all my eagerness to be punctual, I could not get up that staircase. It was a horrible situation, but it was not at its worst even then, for I heard a jarring sound above, as if heavy rusty bolts were being withdrawn.

The Curse was coming down to see what had become of me! I should have to confess my inability to go upstairs without assistance, and so place myself wholly at its mercy!

I made one more desperate effort, and then—and then, upon my word, I don't know how it was exactly—but, as I looked wildly about, I caught sight of my hat on the hat-rack below, and the thoughts it roused in me proved too strong for resistance. Perhaps it was weak of me, but I venture to think that very few men in my position would have behaved any better.

I renounced my ingenious and elaborate scheme for ever, the door (fortunately for me) was neither locked nor bolted, and the next moment I was running for my life along the road to Chelsea, urged on by the fancy that the Curse itself was in hot pursuit.

For weeks after that I lay in hiding, starting at every sound, so fearful was I that the outraged Curse might track me down at last; all my worldly possessions were at Parson's Green, and I could not bring myself to write or call for them, nor indeed have I seen any of the Catafalques since that awful Christmas Eve.

I wish to have nothing more to do with them, for I feel naturally that they took a cruel advantage of my youth and inexperience, and I shall always resent the deception and constraint to which I so nearly fell a victim.

But it occurs to me that those who may have followed my strange story with any curiosity and interest may be slightly disappointed at its conclusion, which I cannot deny is a lame and unsatisfactory one.

They expected, no doubt, to be told what the Curse's personal appearance is, and how it comports itself in that ghastly Grey Chamber, what it said to me, and what I said to it, and what happened after that.

This information, as will be easily understood, I cannot pretend to give, and, for myself, I have long ceased to feel the slightest curiosity on any of these points. But for the benefit of such as are less indifferent, I may suggest that almost any eligible bachelor would easily obtain the opportunities I failed to enjoy by simply calling at the old mansion at Parson's Green, and presenting himself to the baronet as a suitor for his daughter's hand.

I shall be most happy to allow my name to be used as a reference.

## A FAREWELL APPEARANCE

'Andy, come here, sir; I want you.' The little girl who spoke was standing by the table in the morning-room of a London house one summer day, and she spoke to a small silver-grey terrier lying curled up at the foot of one of the window curtains.

As Dandy happened to be particularly comfortable just then, he pretended not to hear, in the hope that his child-mistress would not press the point.

But she did not choose to be trifled with in this way: he was called more imperiously still, until he could dissemble no longer and came out gradually, stretching himself and yawning with a deep sense of injury.

'I know you haven't been asleep; I saw you watching the flies,' she said. 'Come up here, on the table.'

Seeing there was no help for it, he obeyed, and sat down on the table-cloth opposite to her, with his tongue hanging out and his eyes blinking, waiting her pleasure.

Dandy was rather particular as to the hands he allowed to touch him, but generally speaking, he found it pleasant enough (when he had nothing better to do) to resign himself to be pulled about, lectured, or caressed by Hilda.

She was a strikingly pretty child, with long curling brown locks, and a petulant profile, which reminded one of Mr. Doyle's charming wilful little fairy princesses.

On the whole, although Dandy privately considered she had taken rather a liberty in disturbing him, he was willing to overlook it.

'I've been thinking, Dandy,' said Hilda, reflectively, 'that as you and Lady Angelina will be thrown a good deal together when we go into the country next week, you ought to know one another, and you've never been properly introduced yet; so I'm going to introduce you now.'

Now Lady Angelina was only Hilda's doll, and a doll, too, with perhaps as few ideas as any doll ever had yet—which is a good deal to say.

Dandy despised her with all the enlightenment of a thoroughly superior dog; he considered there was simply nothing in her, except possibly bran, and it had made him jealous and angry for a long time to notice the influence that this staring, simpering creature had managed to gain over her mistress.

'Now sit up,' said Hilda. Dandy sat up. He felt that committed him to nothing, but he was careful not to look at Lady Angelina, who was lolling ungracefully in the work-basket with her toes turned in.

'Lady Angelina,' said Hilda next, with great ceremony, 'let me introduce my particular friend Mr. Dandy. Dandy, you ought to bow and say something nice and clever, only you can't; so you must give Angelina your paw instead.'

Here was an insult for a self-respecting dog! Dandy determined never to disgrace himself by presenting his paw to a doll; it was quite against his principles. He dropped on all fours rebelliously.

'That's very rude of you,' said Hilda, 'but you shall do it. Angelina will think it so odd of you. Sit up again and give your paw, and let Angelina stroke your head.'

The dog's little black nose wrinkled and his lips twitched, showing his sharp white teeth: he was not going to be touched by Angelina's flabby wax hand if he could help it!

Unfortunately, Hilda, like older people sometimes, was bent upon forcing persons to know one another, in spite of an obvious unwillingness on at least one side, and so she brought the doll up to the terrier, and, taking one limp pink arm, attempted to pat the dog's head with it.

This was too much: his eyes flamed red like two signal lamps, there was a sharp sudden snap, and the next minute Lady Angelina's right arm was crunched viciously between Dandy's keen teeth.

After that there was a terrible pause. Dandy knew he was in for it, but he was not sorry. He dropped the mangled pieces of wax one by one, and stood there with his head on one side, growling to himself, but wincing for all that, for he was afraid to meet Hilda's indignant grey eyes.

'You abominable, barbarous dog!' she said at last, using the longest words she could to impress him. 'See what you've done! you've bitten poor Lady Angelina's arm off.'

He could not deny it; he had. He looked down at the fragments before him, and then sullenly up again at Hilda. His eyes said what he felt—'I'm glad of it—serves her right; I'd do it again.'

'You deserve to be well whipped,' continued Hilda, severely; 'but you do howl so. I shall leave you to your own conscience' (a favourite remark of her governess) 'until your bad heart is touched, and you come here and say you're sorry and beg both our pardons. I only wish you could be made to pay for a new arm. Go away out of my sight, you bad dog; I can't bear to look at you!'

Dandy, still impenitent, moved leisurely down from the table and out of the open door into the kitchen. He was thinking that Angelina's arm was very nasty, and he should like something to take the taste away. When he got downstairs, however, he found the butcher was calling and had left the area gate open, which struck him as a good opportunity for a ramble. By the time he came back Hilda would have forgotten all about it, or she might think he was lost, and find out which was the more valuable animal—a silly, useless doll, or an intelligent dog like himself.

Hilda saw him from the window as he bolted out with tail erect. 'He's doing it to show off,' she said to herself; 'he's a horrid dog sometimes. But I suppose I shall have to forgive him when he comes back!'

However, Dandy did not come back that night, nor all next day, nor the day after that, nor any more; for the fact was, an experienced dog-stealer had long had his eye upon him, and Dandy happened to come across him that very morning.

He was not such a stupid dog as to be unaware he was doing wrong in following a stranger, but then the man had such delightful suggestions about him of things dogs love to eat, and Dandy had started for his run in a disobedient temper.

So he followed the broken-nosed, bandy-legged man till they reached a narrow lonely alley, and then just as Dandy was thinking about going home again, the stranger turned suddenly on him, hemmed him up in a corner, caught him dexterously up in one hand, tapped him sharply on the head, and slipped him, stunned, into a capacious inside pocket.

'I thought werry likely I should come on you in 'ere, Bob,' said a broken-nosed man in a fur cap, about a week after Dandy's disappearance, to a short, red-faced, hoarse man who was drinking at the bar of a public-house.

'Ah,' said the hoarse man; 'well, you ain't fur out as it happens.'

'Yes, I did,' said the other. 'I met your partner the other day, and he tells me you're looking out for a noo Toby dawg. I've got a article somewheres about me at this moment I should like you to cast a eye over.'

And, diving into his inside pocket he fished out a small shining silver-grey terrier which he slammed down rather roughly on the pewter counter.

Of course the terrier was Hilda's lost Dandy. For some reason or other, the dog-stealer had not thought it prudent to claim the reward offered for him as he had intended to do at first, and Dandy, not being of a breed in fashionable demand, the man was trying to get rid of him now for the best price he could obtain from humble purchasers.

'Well, we do want a understudy, and that's a fact,' said the hoarse man, who was one of the managers of Mr. Punch's Theatre. 'The Toby as travels with us now is breakin' up, getting so blind he don't know Punch from Jack Ketch. But that there animal 'ud never make a 'it as a Toby,' he said, examining Dandy critically: 'why, that's bin a gen'leman's dawg once, that has—we don't want no amatoors on our show.'

'It's the amatoors as draws nowadays,' said the dog-fancier: 'not but what this 'ere partic'lar dawg has his gifts for the purfession. You see him sit up and smoke a pipe and give yer his paw, now.'

And he put Dandy through these performances on the sloppy counter. It was much worse than being introduced to Angelina; but hunger and fretting and rough treatment had broken down the dog's spirit, and it was with dull submission now that he repeated the poor little tricks Hilda had taught him with such pretty perseverance.

'It's no use talking,' said the showman, though he began to show some signs of yielding. 'It takes a tyke born and bred to make a reg'lar Toby. And this ain't a young dog, and he ain't 'ad no proper dramatic eddication; he's not worth to us not the lowest you'd take for him.'

'Well now, I'll tell you 'ow fur I'm willing to meet yer,' said the other persuasively; 'you shall have him, seein' it's you, for—' And so they haggled on for a little longer, but at the end of the interview Dandy had changed hands, and was permanently engaged as a member of Mr. Punch's travelling company.

A few days after that Dandy made acquaintance with his strange fellow-performers. The men had put the show up on a deserted part of a common near London, behind the railings of a little cemetery where no one was likely to interfere with them, and the new Toby was hoisted up on the very narrow and uncomfortable shelf to go through his first interview with Mr. Punch.

When that popular gentleman appeared at his side Dandy examined him with pricked and curious ears. He was rather odd-looking, but his smile, though there was certainly a good deal of it, seemed genial and encouraging, and the poor dog wagged his tail in a conciliatory manner—he wanted some one to be kind to him again.

'The dawg's a fool, Bob,' growled Jem, the other proprietor of the show, a little shabby dirty-faced man with a thin and ragged red beard, who was watching the experiment from the outside; 'he's a-waggin' his bloomin' tail—he'll be a-lickin of Punch's face next! Try him with a squeak.'

And Bob produced a sound which was a hideous compound of chuckle, squeak, and crow, when Dandy, in the full persuasion that the strange figure must be a new variety of cat, flew at it blindly.

But though he managed to get a firm grip of its great hook nose, there was not much satisfaction to be got out of that—the hard wood made his teeth ache, and besides, in his excitement he overbalanced himself and came suddenly down upon Mr. Robert Blott inside, who swore horribly and put him up again.

Then, after a little highly mysterious dancing up and down, and wagging his head, Mr. Punch, in the most uncalled-for manner, hit Dandy over the head with a stick, in order, as Jem put it, 'to get up a ill-feeling between them'—a wanton insult that made the dog madder than ever.

He did not revenge himself at once: he only barked furiously and retreated to his corner of the stage; but the next time Punch came sidling cautiously up to him, Dandy made, not for his wooden head, but for a place between his shoulders which he thought looked more yielding.

There was a savage howl from below, Punch dropped in a heap on the narrow shelf, and Mr. Blott sucked his finger and thumb with many curses.

Mr. Punch was not killed, however, though Dandy had at first imagined he had settled him. He revived almost directly, when he proceeded to rain down such a shower of savage blows from his thick stick upon every part of the dog's defenceless body, that Dandy was completely subdued long before his master thought fit to leave off.

By the time the lesson came to an end, Dandy was sore and shaken and dazed, for Bob had allowed himself to be a little carried away by personal feeling. Still it only showed Dandy more plainly that Mr. Punch was not a person to be trifled with, and, though he liked him as little as ever, he respected as well as feared him.

Unfortunately for Dandy, he was a highly intelligent terrier, of an inquiring turn of mind, and so, after he had been led about for some days with the show, and was able to think things over and put them together, he began to suspect that Punch and the other figures were not alive after all, but only a particularly ugly set of dolls, which Mr. Blott put in motion in some way best known to himself.

From the time he was perfectly certain of this he felt a degraded dog indeed. He had scorned once to allow himself to be even touched by Angelina (who at least was not unpleasant to look at, and always quite inoffensive): now, every hour of his life he found himself ordered about and insulted before a crowd of shabby strangers by a vulgar tawdry doll, to which he was obliged to be civil and even affectionate—as if it was something real!

Dandy was an honest dog, and so, of course, it was very revolting to his feelings to have to impose upon the public in this manner; but Mr. Punch, if he was only a doll, had a way of making himself obeyed.

And though in time the new Toby learnt to perform his duties respectably enough, he did so without the least enthusiasm: it wounded his pride—besides making him very uncomfortable—when Punch caught hold of his head, and something with red whiskers and a blue frock took him by the hind legs, and danced jerkily round the stage with him. He hated that more than anything. Day by day he grew more miserable and homesick.

He loathed the Punch and Judy show and every doll in it, from the hero down to the ghost and the baby. Jem and Bob were not actually unkind to him, and would even have been friendly had he allowed it; but he was a dainty dog, with a natural dislike to ill-dressed and dirty persons, and shrank from their rough if well-meant advances. He never could forget what he had once been, and what he was, and often, in the close sleeping-room of some common lodging-house, he dreamed of the comfortable home he had lost, and Hilda's pretty imperious face, and woke to miss her more than ever.

At first his new masters had been careful to keep him from all chance of escape, and Bob led him after the show by a string; but, as he seemed to be getting resigned to his position, allowed him to run loose.

He was trotting tamely at Jem's heels one hot August morning, followed by a small train of admiring children, when all at once he became aware that he was in a street he knew well—he was near his old home—a few minutes' hard run and he would be safe with Hilda!

He looked up sideways at Jem, who was beating his drum and blowing his pipes, with his eyes on the lower and upper windows. Bob's head was inside the show, and both were in front and not thinking of him just then.

Dandy stopped, turned round upon the unwashed children behind, looked wistfully up at them, as much as to say, 'Don't tell,' and then bolted at the top of his speed.

There was a shrill cry from the children at once of 'Oh, Mr. Punch, sir, please—your dawg's a-runnin' away from yer!' and angry calls to return from the two men. Jem even made an attempt to pursue him, but the drum was too much in his way, and a small dog is not easily caught at the best of times when he takes it into his head to run away. So he gave it up sulkily.

Meanwhile Dandy ran on, till the shouts behind died away. Once an errand boy, struck by the parti-coloured frill round the dog's neck, tried to stop him, but he managed to slip past him and run out into the middle of the road, and kept on blindly, narrowly escaping being run over several times by tradesmen's carts.

And at last, panting and exhausted, he reached the well-remembered gate, out of which he had marched so defiantly, it seemed long ages ago.

The railings were covered with wire netting inside, as he knew, but fortunately some one had left the gate open, and he pattered eagerly down the area steps feeling safe and at home at last.

The kitchen door was shut, but the window was not, and, as the sill was low, he contrived to scramble up somehow and jump into the kitchen, where he reckoned upon finding friends to protect him.

But he found it empty, and looking strangely cold and desolate; only a small fire was smouldering in the range, instead of the cheerful blaze he remembered there, and he could not find the cook—an especial patroness of his—anywhere.

He scampered up into the hall, making straight for the morning-room, where he knew he should find Hilda curled up in one of the arm-chairs with a book.

But that room was empty too—the shutters were up, and the half-light which streamed in above them showed a dreary state of confusion: the writing-table was covered with a sheet and put away in a corner, the chairs were piled up on the centre table, the carpet had been taken up and rolled under the sideboard, and there was a faint warm smell of flue and dust and putty in the place.

He pattered out again, feeling puzzled and a little afraid, and went up the bare stone staircase to find Hilda in one of the upper rooms, perhaps in the nursery.

But the upper rooms, too, were all bare and sheeted and ghostly, and, higher up, the stairs were spotted with great stars of whitewash, and there were ladders and planks on which strange men in dirty white blouses were talking and joking a great deal, and doing a little whitewashing now and then, when they had time for it.

Their voices echoed up and down the stairs with a hollow noise that scared him, and he was afraid to venture any higher. Besides, he knew by this time somehow that Hilda, her father and mother, all the friends he had counted upon seeing again, would not be found in any part of that house.

It was the same house, though stripped and deserted, but all the life and colour and warmth had gone out of it; and he ran here and there, seeking for them in vain.

He picked his way forlornly down to the hall again, and there he found a mouldy old woman with a duster pinned over her head and a dustpan and brush in her hand; for, unhappily for him, the family, servants and all, had gone away some days before into the country, and this old woman had been put into the house as caretaker.

She dropped her brush and pan with a start as she saw him, for she was not fond of dogs.

'Why, deary me,' she said morosely, 'if it hasn't give me quite a turn. However did the nasty little beast get in? a-gallivantin' about as if the 'ole place belonged to him.'

Dandy sat up and begged. In the old days he would not have done such a thing for any servant below a cook (who was always worth being polite to), but he felt a very reduced and miserable little animal indeed just then, and he thought she might be able to take him to Hilda.

But the charwoman's only idea was to get rid of him as quickly as possible.

'Why, if it ain't a Toby dawg!' she cried, as her dim old eyes caught sight of his frill. Here, you get out; you don't belong 'ere!'

And she took him up by the scruff of the neck and went to the front door. As she opened it, a sound came from the street outside which Dandy knew only to well: it was the long-drawn squeak of Mr. Punch.

'That's where he come from, I'll bet a penny,' cried the caretaker, and she went down the steps and called over the gate, 'Hi, master, you don't happen to have lost your Toby dawg, do you? Is this him?'

The man with the drum came up—it was Jem himself; and thereupon Dandy was ignominiously handed over the railings to him, and delivered up once more to the hard life he had so nearly succeeded in shaking off.

He had a severe beating when they got him home, as a warning to him not to rebel again; and he never did try to run away a second time. Where was the good of it? Hilda was gone he did not know where, and the house was a home no longer.

So he went patiently about with the show, a dismal little dog-captive, the dullest little Toby that ever delighted a street audience; so languid and listless at times that Mr. Punch was obliged to rap him really hard on the head before he could induce him to take the slightest notice of him.

But in spite of all this, he made the people laugh; most, perhaps, at night, when the show was lit up by a flaring can of paraffin, and he sat with his feet in Punch's coffin, howling dolefully at the melancholy strains of Jem's pipes, which Dandy always found too much for his feelings.

It was winter time, about a fortnight after Christmas, and the night was snowy and slushy outside, though warm enough in the kitchen of a big Belgravian house. The kitchen was crowded, a stream of waiters and gorgeous powdered footmen and smart maids was perpetually coming and going; in front of the fire a tired little terrier, with a shabby frill round his neck, was basking in the blaze, and near him sat a little dirty-faced man with a red beard, who was being listened to with some attention by a few of the upper servants, who were enjoying a moment's leisure.

'Yes,' he was saying, 'I've been in the purfession a sight o' years now, but I don't know as I ever heard on a Punch's show like me and my mate's bein' engaged for a reg'lar swell evenin' party afore. It shows, to my mind, as public taste is a-coming round—it ain't quite so low as formerly.'

The little man was Jem; and he, with his partner Bob, and Dandy, were in the house owing to an eccentric notion of its master, who happened to have a taste for experiments.

He agreed with many who consider that some kind of amusement in the intervals of dancing is welcome to children; but it was one of his ideas too that they must be getting a little bored by the inevitable lecture with the dissolving views, and find a conjuror (even after seeing him several times in a fortnight) as a rule more bewildering than amusing; although as a present-producing animal, the last has his compensations.

He was curious to see whether the drama of Punch and Judy had quite lost its old power to please. He could easily have hired an elegant and perfectly refined form of the entertainment from some of the fashionable toy-shops or 'universal providers,' only unfortunately in these improved versions much of the original fun is often found to have been refined away.

So he had decided upon introducing the original Mr. Punch from his native streets and in his natural uncivilised state, and Jem and Bob chanced to be the persons selected to exhibit him.

'Juveniles is all alike,' observed the butler, who, having been commissioned to engage the showmen, condescended to feel a fatherly interest in the affair; ''igh or low, there's nothing pleases 'em more than seeing one party a-fetching another party a thunderin' good whack over the 'ead. That's where, in my opinion, all these pantomimes makes a mistake. There's too much bally and music 'all about 'em and not 'arf enough buttered slide and red-'ot poker.'

'There's plenty of 'ead whackin' in our show,' said Jem, with some pride, 'for my partner, you see, he don't find as the dialogue come as fluid to him as he could wish for, so he cuts a deal of it, and what ain't squeakin' is mostly stick—like a cheap operer.'

'Your little dog seems very wet and tired,' said a pretty housemaid, bending down to pat Dandy, as he lay stretched out wearily at her feet. 'Would he eat a cake if I got one for him?'

'He ain't, not to say, fed on cakes as a general thing,' said Jem drily, 'but you can try him, miss, and thankee.'

But Dandy only half raised his head and rejected the cake languidly—he was very comfortable there in the warm firelight, and the place made him feel as if he were back in his own old kitchen, but he was too tired to be hungry.

'He won't hardly look at it,' said the housemaid compassionately. 'I don't think he can be well.'

'Well!' said Jem. 'He's well enough; that's all his contrariness, that is. The fact is, he thinks hisself a deal too good for the likes of us, he do—thinks he ought to be kep' on chickin in a droring-room!' he sneered, wasting his satire on the unconscious Dandy.

'I tell you what it is, miss: that there dawg's 'art ain't in his business—he reg'lar looks down on the 'ole concern, thinks it low! Why, I see 'im from the werry fust a-turnin' up his nose at it, and it downright set me against him. Give me a Toby as takes a interest in the drama! The last but one as we had, afore him, now, he used to look on from start to finish, and when Punch went and 'anged Jack Ketch, why, that dawg used to bark and jump about as pleased as Punch 'isself, and he'd go in among the crowd too and fetch back the babby as Punch pitched out o' winder, as tender with it as a Newfunland! And he warn't like the general run of Tobies neither, for he got quite thick with the Punch figger—thought a deal on 'im, he did—and if you'll believe me, when I 'ad to get the figger a noo 'ead and costoom, it broke the dawg's 'art—he pined away quite rapid. But this 'ere one wouldn't turn a 'air if the 'ole company went to blazes together!'

Here Bob, who had been setting up the show in one of the rooms, came into the kitchen, looking rather uneasy at finding himself in such fine company, and Dandy was spared further upbraidings, as he was called upon to follow the pair upstairs.

They went up into a large handsome room, where at one end there were placed rows of rout seats and chairs, and at the other the homely old show, seeming oddly out of place in its new surroundings.

Poor draggled Dandy felt more ashamed of it and himself than ever, and he was glad to get away under its ragged hangings and lie still by Bob's dirty boots till he was wanted.

And then there was the sound of children's voices and laughter as they all came trooping in, with a crisp rustle of delicate dresses and a scent of hothouse flowers and kid gloves, that reached Dandy where he lay: it reminded him of evenings long ago when Hilda had had parties, and he had been washed and combed and decked out in ribbons for the occasion, and children had played with him and given him nice things to eat—they had generally disagreed with him, but now he could only remember the pleasure and petting of it all.

He would not be petted any more! Presently these children would see him smoking a pipe and being familiar with that low Punch. They would laugh at him too—they always did—and Dandy, like most dogs, hated being laughed at, and never took it as a compliment.

The host's experiment was evidently a complete success: the children, even the most blasés, who danced the newest valse step and thought pantomines vulgar, were delighted to meet an old friend so unexpectedly. A good many had often yearned to see the whole show right through from beginning to end, and chance or a stern nurse had never permitted it. Now their time had come, and Mr. Punch, in spite of his lamentable shortcomings in every relation of life, was received with the usual uproarious applause.

At last the hero called for his faithful dog Toby, as a distraction after the painful domestic scenes, in which he had felt himself driven to throw his child out of window and silence the objections of his wife by becoming a widower, and accordingly Dandy was caught up and set on the shelf by his side.

The sudden glare hurt his eyes, and he sat there blinking at the audience with a pitiful want of pride in his dignity as Dog Toby.

He tried to look as if he didn't know Punch, who was doing all he could to catch his eye, for his riotous 'rootitoot' made him shiver nervously, and long to get away from the whole thing and lie down somewhere in peace.

Jem was scowling up at him balefully. 'I know'd that 'ere dawg would go and disgrace hisself,' he was saying to himself. 'When I get him to myself, he shall catch it for this!'

Dandy was able to see better now, and he found, as he had guessed, that here was not one of his usual audiences—no homely crowd of loitering errand boys, smirched maids-of-all-work, and ragged children jostling and turning their grinning white faces up to him.

There were children here too—plenty of them—but children at their best and daintiest, and looking as if untidiness and quarrels were things unknown to them—though possibly they were not. The laughter, however, was much the same as he was accustomed to, more musical perhaps, and pleasanter to hear, but quite as hearty and unrestrained—they were laughing at him, and he hung his head abashed.

But all at once he forgot his shame, though he did not remember Mr. Punch a bit the more for that; he ran backwards and forwards on his ledge, sniffing and whining, wagging his tail and giving short piteous barks in a state of the wildest excitement. The reason of it was this: near the end of the front row he saw a little girl who was bending eagerly forward with her pretty grey eyes wide open and a puzzled line on her forehead.

Dandy knew her at the very first glance. It was Hilda, looking more like a fairy princess than ever.

She knew him almost as soon, for her clear voice rang out above the general laughter. 'Oh, that isn't Toby—he's my own dog, my Dandy, that I lost! It is really; let him come to me, please do! Don't you see how badly he wants to?'

There was a sudden surprised silence at this—even Mr. Punch was quiet for an instant; but as soon as Dandy heard her voice he could wait no longer, and crouched for a spring.

'Catch the dog, somebody, he's going to jump!' cried the master of the house, more amused than ever, from behind.

Jem was too sulky to interfere, but some good-natured grown-up person caught the trembling dog just in time to save him from a broken leg, or worse, and handed him to his delighted little mistress; and I think the frantic joy which Dandy felt as he was clasped tight in her loving arms once more and covered her flushed face with his eager kisses more than made up for all he had suffered.

Hilda scornfully refused to have anything to do with Jem, who tried hard to convince her she was mistaken. She took her recovered favourite to her hostess.

'He really is mine!' she assured her earnestly; and he doesn't want to be a Toby, I'm sure he doesn't: see how he trembles when that horrid man comes near. Dear Mrs. Lovibond, please tell them I'm to have him!'

And of course Hilda carried her point, for the showmen were not unwilling, after a short conversation with the master of the house, to give up their rights in a dog who would never be much of an ornament to their profession, and was out of health into the bargain.

Hilda held Dandy, all muddy and draggled as he was, fast in her arms all through the remainder of the performance, as if she was afraid Mr. Punch might still claim him for his own; and the dog lay there in measureless content. The hateful squeak made him start and shiver no more; he was too happy to howl at Jem's dismal pipes and drum: they had no terrors for him any more.

'I think I should like to go home now,' she said to her hostess, when Mr. Punch had finally retired. 'Dandy is so excited; feel how his heart beats, just there, you know; he ought to be in bed, and I want to tell them all at home so much!'

She resisted all despairing entreaties to stay, from several small partners who felt life a blank after she had gone—till supper came; and so her carriage was called, and she and Dandy drove home in it together once more.

'Dandy, you're very quiet,' she said once, as they bowled easily and swiftly along. 'Aren't you going to tell me you're glad to be mine again?'

But Dandy could only wag his tail feebly and look up in her face with an exhausted sigh. He had suffered much and was almost worn out; but rest was coming to him at last.

As soon as the carriage had stopped and the door was opened, Hilda ran in, breathless with excitement.

'Oh, Parker, look!' she cried to the maid in the hall, 'Dandy is found—he's here!'

The maid took the lifeless little body from her, looked at it for a moment under the lamp, and turned away without speaking. Then she placed it gently in Hilda's arms again.

'Oh, Miss Hilda, didn't you see?' she said, with a catch in her voice. 'Don't take on, now; but it's come too late—poor little dog, he's gone!'


ACCOMPANIED ON THE FLUTE

A TALE OF ANCIENT ROME

The Consul Duilius was entering Rome in triumph after his celebrated defeat of the Carthaginian fleet at Mylæ. He had won a great naval victory for his country with the first fleet that it had ever possessed—which was naturally a gratifying reflection, and he would have been perfectly happy now, if he had only been a little more comfortable.

But he was standing in an extremely rickety chariot, which was crammed with his nearer relations and a few old friends, to whom he had been obliged to send tickets. At his back stood a slave who held a heavy Etruscan crown on the Consul's head, and whenever he thought his master was growing conceited, threw in the reminder that he was only a man after all—a liberty which at any other time he might have had good reason to regret.

Then the large Delphic wreath, which Duilius wore as well as the crown, had slipped down over one eye and was tickling his nose, while—as both his hands were occupied, one with a sceptre, the other with a laurel bough, and he had to hold on tightly to the rail of the chariot whenever it jolted—there was nothing to do but suffer in silence.

They had insisted, too, upon painting him a beautiful bright red all over, and though it made him look quite new, and very shining and splendid, he had his doubts at times whether it was altogether becoming, and particularly, whether he would ever be able to get it off again.

But these were but trifles after all, and nothing compared with the honour and glory of it! Was not everybody straining to catch a glimpse of him? Did not even the spotted and skittish horses which drew the chariot repeatedly turn round to gaze upon his vermilioned features? As Duilius remarked this, he felt that he was, indeed, the central personage in all this magnificence, and that, on the whole, he liked it.

He could see the beaks of the ships he had captured, bobbing up and down in the middle distance; he could see the white bulls destined for sacrifice entering completely into the spirit of the thing, and redeeming the procession from any monotony by occasionally bolting down a back street, or tossing on their gilded horns some of the flamens who were walking solemnly in front of them.

He could hear, too, above five distinct brass bands, the remarks of his friends as they predicted rain, or expressed a pained surprise at the smallness of the crowd and the absence of any genuine enthusiasm; and he caught the general purport of the very offensive ribaldry circulated at his own expense among the brave legions that brought up the rear.

This was merely the usual course of things on such occasions, and a great compliment when properly understood, and Duilius felt it to be so. In spite of his friends, and the red paint, and the familiar slave, in spite of the extreme heat of the weather and his itching nose, he told himself that this—and this alone—was worth living for.

And it was a painful reflection to him that, after all, it would only last a day: he could not go on triumphing like this for the remainder of his natural life—he would not be able to afford it on his moderate income; and yet—and yet—existence would fall woefully flat after so much excitement.

It may be supposed that Duilius was naturally fond of ostentation and notoriety, but this was far from being the case; on the contrary, at ordinary times his disposition was retiring and almost shy; but his sudden success had worked a temporary change in him, and in the very flush of triumph he found himself sighing to think that, in all human probability, he would never go about with trumpeters and trophies, with flute-players and white oxen, any more in his whole life.

And then he reached the Porta Triumphalis, where the chief magistrates and the Senate awaited them, all seated upon spirited Roman-nosed chargers, which showed a lively emotion at the approach of the procession, and caused some of their riders to dismount, with as much affectation of method and design as their dignity enjoined and the nature of the occasion permitted.

There Duilius was presented with the freedom of the City and an address, which last he put in his pocket, as he explained, to read at home.

And then an Ædile informed him in a speech, during which he twice lost his notes and had to be prompted by a lictor, that the grateful Republic, taking into consideration the Consul's distinguished services, had resolved to disregard expense, and on that auspicious day to give him whatever reward he might choose to demand—'in reason,' the Ædile added cautiously, as he quitted his saddle with an unexpectedness which scarcely seemed intentional.

Duilius was naturally a little overwhelmed by such liberality, and, like everyone else favoured suddenly with such an opportunity, was quite incapable of taking complete advantage of it.

For a time he really could not remember in his confusion anything he would care for at all, and he thought it might look mean to ask for money.

At last he recalled his yearning for a Perpetual Triumph, but his natural modesty made him moderate, and he could not find courage to ask for more than a fraction of the glory that now attended him.

So, not without some hesitation, he replied that they were exceedingly kind, and since they left it entirely to his discretion, he would like—if they had no objection—he would like a flute-player to attend him whenever he went out.

Duilius very nearly asked for a white bull as well; but, on second thoughts, he felt it might lead to inconvenience, and there were many difficulties connected with the proper management of such an animal; the Consul, from what he had seen that day, felt that it would be imprudent to trust himself in front of the bull—while, if he walked behind, he might be mistaken for a cattle-driver, which would be odious. And so he gave up that idea, and contented himself with a simple flute-player.

The Senate, visibly relieved by so very unassuming a request, granted it with positive effusion; Duilius was invited to select his musician, and chose the biggest, after which the procession moved on through the Arch and up the Capitoline Hill, while the Consul had time to remember things he would have liked even better than a flute-player, and to suspect dimly that he might have made rather an ass of himself.

That night Duilius was entertained at a supper given at the public expense; he went out with the proud resolve to show his sense of the compliment paid him by scaling the giddiest heights of intoxication. The Romans of that day only drank wine and water at their festivals, but it is astonishing how inebriated a person of powerful will can become—even on wine and water—if he only gives his mind to it. And Duilius, being a man of remarkable determination, returned from that hospitable board particularly drunk; the flute-player saw him home, however, helped him to bed, though he could not induce him to take off his sandals, and lulled him to a heavy slumber by a selection from the popular airs of the time.

So that the Consul, although he awoke late next day with a bad headache and a perception of the vanity of most things, still found reason to congratulate himself upon his forethought in securing so invaluable an attendant, and planned, rather hopefully, sundry little ways of making him useful about the house.

As the subsequent history of this great naval commander is examined with the impartiality that becomes the historian, it is impossible to be blind to the melancholy fact that, in the first flush of his elation, Duilius behaved with an utter want of tact and taste that must have gone far to undermine his popularity, and proved a source of much gratification to his friends.

He would use that flute-player everywhere—he overdid the thing altogether: for example, he used to go out to pay formal calls, and leave the flute-player in the hall, tootling to such an extent that at last his acquaintances were forced in self-defence to deny themselves to him.

When he attended worship at the temples, too, he would bring the flute-player with him, on the flimsy pretext that he could assist the choir during service; and it was the same at the theatres, where Duilius—such was his arrogance—actually would not take a box unless the manager admitted his flute-player to the orchestra and guaranteed him at least one solo between the acts.

And it was the Consul's constant habit to strut about the Forum with his musician executing marches behind him, until the spectacle became so utterly ridiculous that even the Romans of that age, who were as free from the slightest taint of humour as a self-respecting nation can possibly be, began to notice something peculiar.

But the day of retribution dawned at last. Duilius worked the flute so incessantly that the musician's stock of airs was very soon exhausted, and then he was naturally obliged to blow them all through once more.

The excellent Consul had not a fine ear, but even he began to hail the fiftieth repetition of 'Pugnare nolumus,' for instance—the great national peace anthem of the period—with the feeling that he had heard the same tune at least twice before, and preferred something slightly fresher, while others had taken a much shorter time in arriving at the same conclusion.

The elder Duilius, the Consul's father, was perhaps the most annoyed by it; he was a nice old man in his way—the glass and china way—but he was a typical old Roman, with a manly contempt for pomp, vanity, music, and the fine arts generally.

So that his son's flute-player, performing all day in the court-yard, drove the old gentleman nearly mad, until he would rush to the windows and hurl the lighter articles of furniture at the head of the persistent musician, who, however, after dodging them with dexterity, affected to treat them as a recognition of his efforts, and carried them away gratefully to sell.

Duilius senior would have smashed the flute, only it was never laid aside for a single instant, even at meals; he would have made the player drunk and incapable, but he was a member of the Manus Spei, and he would with cheerfulness have given him a heavy bribe to go away, if the honest fellow had not proved absolutely incorruptible.

So he could only sit down and swear, and then relieve his feelings by giving his son a severe thrashing, with threats to sell him for whatever he might fetch: for, in the curious conditions of ancient Roman society, a father possessed both these rights, however his offspring might have distinguished himself in public life.

Naturally, Duilius did not like the idea of being put up to auction, and he began to feel that it was slightly undignified for a Roman general who had won a naval victory and been awarded a first-class Triumph to be undergoing corporal punishment daily at the hands of an unflinching parent, and accordingly he determined to go and expostulate with his flute-player.

He was beginning to find him a nuisance himself, for all his old shy reserve and unwillingness to attract attention had returned to him; he was fond of solitude, and yet he could never be alone; he was weary of doing everything to slow music, like the bold bad man in a melodrama.

He could not even go across the street to purchase a postage-stamp without the flute-player coming stalking out after him, playing away like a public fountain; while, owing to the well-known susceptibility of a rabble to the charm of music, the disgusted Consul had to take his walks abroad at the head of Rome's choicest scum.

Duilius, with a lively recollection of these inconveniences, would have spoken very seriously indeed to his musician, but he shrank from hurting his feelings by the plain truth. He simply explained that he had not intended the other to accompany him always, but only on special occasions; and, while professing the sincerest admiration for his musical proficiency, he felt, as he said, unwilling to monopolise it, and unable to enjoy it at the expense of a fellow-creature's rest and comfort.

Perhaps he put the thing a little too delicately to secure the object he had in view, for the musician, although he was obviously deeply touched by such unwonted consideration, waived it aside with a graceful fervour that was quite irresistible.

He assured the Consul that he was only too happy to have been selected to render his humble tribute to the naval genius of so eminent a commander; he would not admit that his own rest and comfort were in the least affected by his exertions, for, being naturally fond of the flute, he could, he protested, perform upon it continuously for whole days without fatigue. And he concluded by pointing out very respectfully that for the Consul to dispense, even to a small extent, with an honour decreed (at his own particular request) by the Republic, would have the appearance of ingratitude, and expose him to the gravest suspicions. After which he rendered the ancient love chant 'Ludus idem, ludus vetus,' with singular sweetness and expression.

Duilius felt the force of his arguments: Republics are proverbially forgetful, and he was aware that it might not be safe, even for him, to risk offending the Senate.

So he had nothing to do but just go on, and be followed about by the flute-player, and castigated by his parent in the old familiar way, until he had very little self-respect left.

At last he found a distraction in his care-laden existence—he fell deeply in love. But even here a musical Nemesis attended him, to his infinite embarrassment, in the person of his devoted follower. Sometimes Duilius would manage to elude him and slip out unseen to some sylvan retreat, where he had reason to hope for a meeting with the object of his adoration. He generally found that in this expectation he had not deceived himself; but always, just as he had found courage to speak of the passion that consumed him, a faint tune would strike his ear from afar, and, turning his head in a fury, he would see his faithful flute-player striding over the fields in pursuit of him with unquenchable ardour.

He gave in at last, and submitted to the necessity of speaking all his tender speeches 'through music.' Claudia did not seem to mind it, perhaps finding an additional romance in being wooed thus, and Duilius himself, who was not eloquent, found that the flute came in very well at awkward pauses in the conversation.

Then they were married, and, as Claudia played very nicely herself upon the tibiæ, she got up musical evenings, when she played duets with the flute-player, which Duilius, if he had only had a little more taste for music, might have enjoyed immensely.

As it was, beginning to observe for the first time that the musician was far from uncomely, he forbade the duets. Claudia wept and sulked, and Claudia's mother said that Duilius was behaving like a brute, and she was not to mind him; but the harmony of their domestic life was broken, until the poor Consul was driven to take long country walks in sheer despair, not because he was fond of walking, for he hated it, but simply to keep the flute-player out of mischief.

He was now debarred from all other society, for his old friends had long since cut him dead whenever he chanced to meet them. 'How could he expect people to stop and talk,' they asked indignantly, 'when there was that confounded fellow blowing tunes down the backs of their necks all the time?'

Duilius had had enough of it himself, and felt this so strongly that one day he took his flute-player a long walk through a lonely wood, and, choosing a moment when his companion had played 'Id omnes faciunt' till he was somewhat out of breath, he turned on him suddenly. When he left the lonely wood he was alone, and somewhere in the undergrowth lay a broken flute, and near it something which looked as if it might once have been a musician.

The Consul went home and sat there waiting for the deed to become generally known. He waited with a certain uneasiness, because it was impossible to tell how the Senate might take the thing, or the means by which their vengeance would declare itself.

And yet his uneasiness was counterbalanced by a delicious relief: the State might disgrace, banish, put him to death even, but he had got rid of slow music for ever; and as he thought of this, the stately Duilius would snap his fingers and dance with secret delight.

All disposition to dance, however, was forgotten upon the arrival of lictors bearing an official missive. He looked at it for a long time before he dared to break the big seal and cut the cord which bound the tablets which might contain his doom.

He did it at last, and smiled with relief as he began to read; for the decree was courteously, almost affectionately, worded. The Senate, considering (or affecting to consider) the disappearance of the flute-player a mere accident, expressed their formal regret at the failure of the provision made in his honour.

Then, as he read on, Duilius dashed the tablets into small fragments, and rolled on the ground, and tore his hair, and howled: for the Senatorial decree concluded by a declaration that, in consideration of his brilliant exploits, the State thereby placed at his disposal two more flute-players, who, it was confidently hoped, would survive the wear and tear of their ministrations longer than the first.

Duilius retired to his room and made his will, taking care to have it properly signed and attested. Then he fastened himself in, and when they broke down the door next day, they found a lifeless corpse, with a strange sickly smile upon its pale lips.

No one in Rome quite made out the reason of this smile, but it was generally thought to denote the gratification of the deceased at the idea of leaving his beloved ones in comfort, if not luxury; for, though the bulk of his fortune was left to Carthaginian charities, he had had the forethought to bequeath a flute-player apiece to his wife and mother-in-law.

F. Anstey – A Concise Bibliography

Vice Versa (1882)
The Black Poodle And Other Tales (1884)
The Giant's Robe (1884)
The Tinted Venus (1885)
A Fallen Idol (1886)
Burglar Bill And Other Pieces (1888)
The Pariah (1889)
Voces Populi (1890)
Tourmalin's Time Cheques (1891)
Mr. Punch's Model Music-Hall Songs And Dramas (1892)
The Talking Horse And Other Tales (1892)
The Travelling Companions (1892)
The Man From Blankley's And Other Sketches (1893)
Mr. Punch's Pocket Ibsen (1893)
Under the Rose (1894)
Lyre and Lancet (1895)
The Statement of Stella Maberly, Written By Herself (1896)
Baboo Jabberjee, B. A. (1897)
Puppets At Large (1897)
Love Among The Lions (1898)
Paleface And Redskin (1898)
The Brass Bottle (1900)
A Bayard From Bengal (1902)
Only Toys! (1903)
Salted Almonds (1906)
Winnie, An Everyday Story (1909)
In Brief Authority (1915)
Percy and Others (1915)
The Last Load (1925)
The Would-Be Gentleman (Adapted From Molière's Le Bourgeois gentilhomme) (1927)
The Imaginary Invalid (Adapted From Molière's Le Malade imaginaire) (1929)
Humour and Fantasy (1931)
A Long Retrospect (1936)

www.ingramcontent.com/pod-product-compliance
Lightning Source LLC
Chambersburg PA
CBHW071406170626
46811CB00003B/1276